/ CHILDCRAFT

Volume 1
of fifteen volumes

POEMS
AND
RHYMES

CHILDCRAFT

The How and Why Library

FIELD ENTERPRISES EDUCATIONAL CORPORATION
Merchandise Mart Plaza • Chicago 54, Illinois

1964 EDITION
CHILDCRAFT®
The How and Why® *Library*

Copyright © 1964, U.S.A.

by FIELD ENTERPRISES EDUCATIONAL CORPORATION

International Copyright © 1964
by Field Enterprises Educational Corporation
Printed in the United States of America
FDA
LIBRARY OF CONGRESS CATALOG NO. 64-10001

Acknowledgments

The publishers of CHILDCRAFT, *The* How and Why *Library*, gratefully acknowledge the courtesy of the following publishers, agencies, corporations, and authors for permission to use copyrighted poems and illustrations. Full illustration acknowledgments for this volume appear on pages 278 and 279.

Abelard-Schuman, Limited: "Horses" from *Up the Windy Hill*, copyright 1953 by Aileen Fisher
American Oil Company: art page 205, copyright American Oil Company
Anderson, Mildred Leigh: "I Can Be a Tiger" from *Child Life*
D. Appleton-Century Company: "The Little Elf" by John Kendrick Bangs from *St. Nicholas Book of Verse*
Artists and Writers Guild, Inc.: "Open Range" from the Giant Golden Book *Tenggren's Cowboys and Indians* by Kathryn and Byron Jackson, copyright 1948 by Simon and Schuster, Inc. and Artists and Writers Guild, Inc.
Baruch, Dorothy W.: "Stop—Go," "The Elevator," and "Merry-Go-Round" from *I Like Machinery*, copyright 1933 by Harper & Brothers
Bennett, Rowena Bastin: "Four Seasons" reprinted by special permission from *Jack and Jill*
Bobbs-Merrill Company: "The Raggedy Man" from *Rhymes of Childhood* by James Whitcomb Riley, copyright 1890 and 1918 by James Whitcomb Riley
Boyden, Polly Chase: "Mud" from *Child Life*
Brandt & Brandt: "Afternoon on a Hill" from *Collected Poems* by Edna St. Vincent Millay, Harper & Brothers, copyright 1917, 1945 by Edna St. Vincent Millay; "Western Wagons" from *A Book of Americans*, Rinehart & Company, Inc., copyright 1933 by Rosemary and Stephen Vincent Benét
Curtis Brown, Ltd.: "Jonathan Bing" from *Jonathan Bing and Other Verses*, by Beatrice Curtis Brown, copyright 1936 by Beatrice Curtis Brown
Burgess, Gelett: "The Purple Cow" from *The Burgess Nonsense Book*
Jonathan Cape, Limited: "Leisure" from *Collected Poems* by William Henry Davies, reprinted by permission of Mrs. H. M. Davies
Chaffee, Eleanor A.: "The Cobbler" from *American Junior Red Cross News*
Children's Activities magazine publishers: "A New Friend" by Marjorie Allen Anderson
The Cream of Wheat Corp.: photo by Carroll Seghers II, page 90, copyright The Cream of Wheat Corp.
Cullen, Mrs. Ida M.: "Song of the Wake-Up-World" by Countee Cullen
The John Day Company, Inc.: "Skyscraper Is a City's House" from *Skyscraper* by Elsa Naumburg, Clara Lambert, and Lucy Sprague Mitchell, copyright 1933 by The John Day Company, Inc.
Davies, Mary Carolyn: "Drums of the Rain," "The Day Before April," and "Look at the Snow" from *Child Life*
Dodd, Mead & Company: "The Vagabond Song" by Bliss Carmen, courtesy of McClelland and Stewart, Limited, reprinted by special permission of the Bliss Carmen Trust, The University of New Brunswick, Canada; "The World" by William Brighty Rands; "Two Cats of Kilkenny" from *The Little Mother Goose*, compiled by Jessie Wilcox Smith
Doubleday & Company, Inc.: "The Best Game the Fairies Play" and "A Fairy Went A-Marketing" from *Fairies and Chimneys* by Rose Fyleman, copyright 1920 by Doubleday & Company, Inc.; "Daddy," from *Fairies and Friends* by Rose Fyleman, copyright 1926 by Double-

day & Company, Inc.; "Good Night," "Hi-Di," "Hippopotamus," "Mice," and "Sneezes" from *Fifty-One New Nursery Rhymes* by Rose Fyleman, copyright 1932 by Doubleday & Company, Inc.; "Sometimes" from *The Fairy Flute* by Rose Fyleman, copyright 1923 by Doubleday & Company, Inc.; "The Dentist," "Joys," "My Policeman," and "Singing Time" from *The Fairy Green* by Rose Fyleman, copyright 1923 by Doubleday & Company, Inc.; "The New Neighbor" and "October" from *Gay Go Up* by Rose Fyleman, copyright 1930 by Doubleday & Company, Inc., all by courtesy Society of Authors; "Rain in the Night" from *Selected Lyrics* by Amelia Josephine Burr, copyright 1927 by Doubleday & Company, Inc.; "The Animal Store," "Barefoot Days," "Good Green Bus," "The Ice-Cream Man," "I'd Like To Be a Lighthouse," and "Taxis" from *Taxis and Toadstools* by Rachel Field, copyright 1926 by Doubleday & Company, Inc.; "For This New Morning" from *A Little Book of Prayers and Graces* compiled by Quail Hawkins, copyright 1941, 1952 by Doubleday & Company, Inc.; "Sunrise" by Katherine Kosmak from *Creative Youth*, edited by Hughes Mearns, copyright 1925 by Doubleday & Company, Inc.; "Country Trucks" and "Uncle Frank" from *Goose Grass Rhymes* by Monica Shannon, copyright 1930 by Doubleday & Company, Inc.
E. P. Dutton & Co., Inc.: "Galoshes" and "Stars" from the book *Stories To Begin On* by Rhoda W. Bacmeister, copyright 1940 by E. P. Dutton & Co., Inc.; "Dogs," "Drinking Fountain," "In Winter," and "Sliding," copyright 1946 by Marchette Chute; "In August," copyright 1941 by Marchette Chute; and "My Dog" from the book *Around and About* by Marchette Chute, copyright 1932 by Marchette Chute; "Food" and "Mail" from the book *Rhymes About the City* by Marchette Chute, copyright 1946 by Marchette Chute; "Shadow Dance" from the book *Fairies and Suchlike* by Ivy O. Eastwick, copyright 1946 by E. P. Dutton & Co., Inc.; "The End," "Forgiven," and "Furry Bear" from the book *Now We Are Six* by A. A. Milne, copyright 1927 by E. P. Dutton & Co., Inc., renewal 1955 by A. A. Milne, courtesy Methuen & Co., Ltd.; "Halfway Down," "Hoppity," "Puppy and I," "Spring Morning," and "Vespers" from the book *When We Were Very Young* by A. A. Milne, copyright 1924 by E. P. Dutton & Co., Inc., renewal 1952 by A. A. Milne, courtesy Methuen & Co., Ltd.; "Jump or Jiggle" by Evelyn Beyer, "Little Black Bug" by Margaret Wise Brown, "The House of the Mouse" by Lucy Sprague Mitchell, and "My Bed" by Elizabeth Manson Scott, from the book *Another Here and Now Story Book*, compiled by Lucy Sprague Mitchell, copyright 1937 by E. P. Dutton & Co., Inc.
Eastwick, Ivy O.: "May Mornings" reprinted by special permission from *Jack and Jill*
Edelman, Katherine: "Saturday Shopping" from *Child Life*
Fallis, Edwina H.: "September" from *Sung Under the Silver Umbrella*, selected by the Literature Committee of the Association for Childhood Education
Farjeon, Eleanor: "Jumping Rope" by Eleanor Farjeon from *Lavender's Blue* by Kathleen Lines
The First-Stamford National Bank & Trust Company, Stamford, Connecticut: "Dogs and Weather" by Winifred Welles from *Skipping Along Alone*
Fisher, Aileen: "After a Bath" and "Shelling Peas" from *Inside a Little House*; "Otherwise" from *The Coffee-Pot Face*; "December," "I'll Be a Baker," and "Whistling" from *That's Why*
Flexman, John: "The Shiny Little House" by Nancy M. Hayes
Florida Citrus Commission: photo page 95, copyright Florida Citrus Commission
Follett Publishing Company: "Motor Cars" by Rowena Bastin Bennett from *Around a Toadstool Table*, copyright 1930, 1937 by Follett Publishing Company, Chicago, Illinois
Frost, Frances: "Sniff" from *American Junior Red Cross News*
Fyleman, Rose: "The Beech Tree" from *Child Life*
Guiterman, Mrs. Arthur: "Chums" by Arthur Guiterman from *Child Life*
Harcourt, Brace and Company, Inc.: "Circles" and "Trees" from *The Little Hill* by Harry Behn, copyright 1949 by Harry Behn; "Sliding" from *Whispers* by Myra Cohn Livingston, copyright 1958 by Myra Cohn Livingston; "Spring Wind," "When Young Melissa Sweeps," and "Wings and Wheels" from *Magpie Lane* by Nancy Byrd Turner, copyright 1927 by Harcourt, Brace and Company, Inc., renewed 1955 by Nancy Byrd Turner; "A Sunshiny Shower" from *Rainbow in the Sky*, collected and edited by Louis Untermeyer
Harcourt, Brace & World, Inc.: photographs from *The Shadow Book* by Beatrice Schenk de Regniers; photographs copyright 1960 by Isabel Gordon, pages 82 and 83 (*left, top and bottom right*), reproduced by permission of Harcourt, Brace & World, Inc.
Harper & Brothers: "The Mitten Song" and "My Zipper Suit" from *A Pocketful of Rhymes* by Mary Louise Allen, copyright 1939 by Harper & Brothers; "Building a Sky-

CONSULTANTS

The editors and publishers wish to express their appreciation of the outstanding services in planning, consultation, and authentication of CHILDCRAFT, The How and Why Library, *rendered by the following committee of leading educators:*

HOLLIS L. CASWELL, A.B., M.A., Ph.D., LL.D., Pd.D., Chairman. Former President of Teachers College, Columbia University; Now Chairman, Editorial Advisory Boards, Field Enterprises Educational Corporation.

MARY A. ADAMS, B.S., M.A. Assistant Superintendent of Elementary Education, Baltimore, Maryland.

ALICE MIEL, B.A., M.A., Ed.D., LL.D. Head, Department of Curriculum and Teaching, Teachers College, Columbia University.

MAURICE R. AHRENS, A.B., M.A., Ed.D. Professor of Education, University of Florida.

WILLARD C. OLSON, B.A., M.A., Ph.D. Dean of the School of Education, University of Michigan.

MURIEL CROSBY, A.B., M.S., D.Ed. Assistant Superintendent of Schools and Director of Elementary Education, Wilmington, Delaware.

HAROLD G. SHANE, B.E., M.A., Ph.D. Dean of the School of Education, Indiana University.

JOHN I. GOODLAD, Ph.D. Professor of Education, University of California, Los Angeles (U.C.L.A.) and Director of the Laboratory School.

KENNETH D. WANN, B.S., M.A., Ed.D. Professor of Education, Department of Curriculum and Teaching, Teachers College, Columbia University.

Appreciation is also expressed to the following professional leaders for their help in authentication, and for their advice to the editors on specific aspects of CHILDCRAFT, The How and Why Library:

MAE J. DURHAM, B.S. School of Librarianship, University of California, Berkeley.

JEAN THOMSON, B.A., B.S., Boys and Girls Division, Toronto Public Library, Toronto, Ontario, Canada.

JAMES L. HYMES, JR., A.B., M.A., Ed.D. Professor of Education, and Chairman, Early Childhood Education, University of Maryland.

RALPH A. ULVELING, Ph.B., B.S., L.H.D. Director of the Public Library, Detroit, Michigan.

BARBARA S. MOODY, A.B., B.S., L.S. Enoch Pratt Free Library, Baltimore, Maryland.

WILLIAM S. VASILAKES, B.S., M.A. Science Writer, Chicago, Illinois.

R. MARLIN PERKINS, Director, St. Louis Zoo, St. Louis, Missouri.

J. RUSSELL WHITAKER, B.S., M.S., Ph.D. Chairman, Department of Geography, George Peabody College for Teachers.

STAFF

5

a few words about CHILDCRAFT

The pages of CHILDCRAFT will speak for themselves to young children. They will speak of cabbages and kings and many other things, each in an excitingly different way.

The goal of CHILDCRAFT, *The How and Why Library*, is to whet your young child's obvious appetite for learning in several ways:

- By dealing with the questions he most often asks and the curiosities he most often expresses
- By being written in language that is rhythmical, factual, fun to read, and fun to hear
- By organizing information according to his interests rather than according to adult categories
- By arranging text and illustrations so that wherever he turns, he will find a complete and exciting learning unit
- By employing both the latest and the traditional techniques of the graphic arts
- By helping you to help your child in Volumes 14 and 15

Even though CHILDCRAFT is not a textbook nor an encyclopedia, your children will learn from it and find facts in it. And even though CHILDCRAFT is not written like a primer or a basic reader, your children will read better because of it. As you know, the answers they want don't always come in simple, single-syllable words.

Children really want to learn. Learning to do things as well as (or better than) daddy, mother, brother, and sister is a matter of survival for a child. In today's anxious world, it is the difference between being somebody and nobody.

And if the food of knowledge is within reach, if it is attractive, and if it is put before them by loving hands and voices, they will eat of it voraciously. But if it is out of reach—in the top cupboard, or still in the store —their stomach for learning will inevitably shrink. The light of curiosity that burns within them may sputter and remain hidden forever under a bushel of neglect.

In the words of the man to whom this edition of CHILDCRAFT, *The How and Why Library*, is dedicated, the man who was most instrumental in its conception and in its basic development—the late J. Morris Jones, Editor-in-Chief:

"CHILDCRAFT's 5,040 pages are intended to be 5,040 doors to a child's life and learning to come. We hope he opens every one of them, for each door that he opens is sure to delight him now, and also to show him the many doors he still must open to achieve his inalienable destiny—to become a truly human being."

The Editors and Artists

VOLUME 1

CONTENTS

Poems and Rhymes

Volume Layout Artists, Clark Bruorton and Elizabeth Schon

Old Mother Goose, when
She wanted to wander,
Would fly through the air
On a very fine gander.

bye, baby bunting

Bye, baby bunting,
Daddy's gone a-hunting,
To get a little rabbit's skin
To wrap his baby bunting in.

sweeter than sugar

My little baby, little boy blue,
Is as sweet as sugar and cinnamon too;
Isn't this precious darling of ours
Sweeter than dates and cinnamon flowers?

hush, my baby

Hush, li'l baby, don't say a word,
Daddy'll buy you a mockingbird.

When that mockingbird won't sing,
Daddy'll buy you a diamond ring.

When that diamond ring turns to brass,
Daddy'll buy you a looking glass.

When that looking glass gets broke,
Daddy'll buy you a billy goat.

When that billy goat gets bony,
Daddy'll buy you a Shetland pony.

When that pony runs away,
Ta-ra-ra-ra-boom-de-ay.

rock-a-bye, baby

Rock-a-bye, baby, on the treetop,
When the wind blows, the cradle will rock;
When the bough bends, the cradle will fall;
Down will come baby, bough, cradle, and all !

RIDE A COCKHORSE

Ride a cockhorse to Banbury Cross,
   To see a fine lady upon a white horse.
With rings on her fingers,
   And bells on her toes,
She shall have music wherever she goes.

THIS IS THE WAY THE LADIES RIDE

This is the way the ladies ride,
   Tri, tre, tre, tree, tri, tre, tre, tree!
This is the way the ladies ride,
   Tri, tre, tre, tree, tri, tre, tre, tree!

This is the way the gentlemen ride,
   Gallop-a-trot, gallop-a-trot!
This is the way the gentlemen ride,
   Gallop-a-gallop-a-trot!

This is the way the farmers ride,
   Hobbledy-hoy, hobbledy-hoy!
This is the way the farmers ride,
   Hobbledy-hobbledy-hoy!

PAT-A-CAKE

Pat-a-cake, pat-a-cake,
   Baker's man,
Bake me a cake
   As fast as you can.
Pat it and prick it,
   And mark it with a B,
And put it in the oven
   For baby and me.

PEASE PORRIDGE HOT

Pease porridge hot,
   Pease porridge cold,
Pease porridge in the pot,
   Nine days old.
Some like it hot,
   Some like it cold,
Some like it in the pot,
   Nine days old.

RING-AROUND-A-ROSY

Ring-around-a-rosy,
A pocket full of posies;
One, two, three,
And we all fall down!

HAD A MULE

Had a mule, his name was Jack,
    I rode his tail to save his back;
His tail got loose and I fell back-
    Whoa, Jack!

JACK BE NIMBLE

Jack be nimble,
Jack be quick,
And Jack jump over the candlestick.

ONE, TWO,
BUCKLE MY SHOE

One, two,
Buckle my shoe;

Three, four,
Knock at the door;

Five, six,
Pick up sticks;

Seven, eight,
Lay them straight;

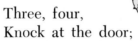

Nine, ten,
A good fat hen.

ONE,
TWO,
THREE,
FOUR,
FIVE

One, two, three, four, five!
I caught a hare alive;
Six, seven, eight, nine, ten!
I let her go again.

SNEEZES

One sneeze is lucky,
Two sneezes queer,
Three sneezes—get your hanky
(Oh, dear, dear),
Four sneezes—off she goes
Into her bed and under the clo'es.

ROSE FYLEMAN

16

SEVEN
BLACKBIRDS
IN A
TREE

Seven blackbirds in a tree,
Count them and see what they be.
One for sorrow
Two for joy
Three for a girl
Four for a boy;
Five for silver
Six for gold
Seven for a secret
That's never been told.

WHAT

ARE

LITTLE

BOYS

MADE

OF?

What are little boys made of, made of?
What are little boys made of?
Snips and snails, and puppy dogs' tails;
And that's what little boys are made of.

What are little girls made of, made of?
What are little girls made of?
Sugar and spice, and all that's nice;
And that's what little girls are made of.

JACK AND JILL

Jack and Jill went up the hill,
To fetch a pail of water;
Jack fell down and broke his crown,
And Jill came tumbling after.

Then up Jack got and home did trot,
As fast as he could caper.
He went to bed to mend his head
With vinegar and brown paper.

GEORGY PORGY

Georgy Porgy, pudding and pie,
Kissed the girls and made them cry;
When the boys came out to play,
Georgy Porgy ran away.

MARY, MARY, QUITE CONTRARY

Mary, Mary, quite contrary,
How does your garden grow?
With cockleshells, and silver bells,
And pretty maids all in a row.

We are all nodding, nid, nid, nodding,
We are all nodding
At our house at home.
With a turning in and a turning out,
And it's this way, that way, round about,
We are all nodding, nid, nid, nodding,
We are all nodding
At our house at home.

WE ARE ALL NODDING

We are all sewing, sew, sew, sewing,
We are all sewing
At our house at home.
With a turning in and a turning out,
And it's this way, that way, round about,
We are all sewing, sew, sew, sewing,
We are all sewing
At our house at home.

We are all fiddling, fid, fid, fiddling,
We are all fiddling
At our house at home.
With a turning in and a turning out,
And it's this way, that way, round about,
We are all fiddling, fid, fid, fiddling,
We are all fiddling
At our house at home.

We are all reading, read, read, reading,
We are all reading
At our house at home.
With a turning in and a turning out,
And it's this way, that way, round about
We are all reading, read, read, reading,
We are all reading
At our house at home.

We are all spinning, spin, spin, spinning,
We are all spinning
At our house at home.
With a turning in and a turning out,
And it's this way, that way, round about,
We are all spinning, spin, spin, spinning,
We are all spinning
At our house at home.

HUMPTY DUMPTY
SAT ON
A WALL

Humpty Dumpty sat on a wall,
Humpty Dumpty had a great fall;
All the King's horses and all the King's men
Couldn't put Humpty Dumpty together again.

24   An Egg

AS I WAS GOING TO ST. IVES

As I was going to St. Ives,
I met a man with seven wives;
Each wife had seven sacks,
Each sack had seven cats,
Each cat had seven kits.
Kits, cats, sacks, and wives,
How many were going to St. Ives?

One

AS WHITE AS MILK

As white as milk,
As soft as silk,
And hundreds close together;
They sail away
On an autumn day,
When windy is the weather.

WILHELMINA SEEGMILLER

Milkweed Seed

LITTLE NANCY ETTICOAT

Little Nancy Etticoat,
In a white petticoat,
And a red nose.
The longer she stands,
The shorter she grows.

A Candle

THIRTY WHITE HORSES

Thirty white horses
On a red hill;
Now they tramp,
Now they champ,
Now they stand still.

The Teeth and Gums

LITTLE BO PEEP

Little Bo-Peep has lost her sheep
    And can't tell where to find them;
Leave them alone, and they'll come home,
    Wagging their tails behind them.

Little Bo-Peep fell fast asleep,
    And dreamed she heard them bleating,
But when she awoke, she found it a joke,
    For still they all were fleeting.

Then she took her little crook,
 Determined for to find them;
She found them indeed, but it made her heart bleed,
 For they'd left their tails behind them.

It happened one day, as Bo-Peep did astray
 Unto a meadow hard by,
There she espied their tails, side by side,
 All hung on a tree to dry.

She heaved a sigh and wiped her eye,
 And ran o'er hill and dale,
And tried what she could, as a shepherdess should,
 To tack each sheep to its tail.

MARY HAD A LITTLE LAMB

Mary had a little lamb,
　Its fleece was white as snow;
And everywhere that Mary went
　The lamb was sure to go.

He followed her to school one day;
　That was against the rule;
It made the children laugh and play
　To see a lamb at school.

SARAH JOSEPHA HALE

PUSSYCAT, PUSSYCAT

Pussycat, pussycat, where have you been?
I've been to London to look at the Queen.
Pussycat, pussycat, what did you there?
I frightened a little mouse under the chair.

JONATHAN

Jonathan Gee
　Went out with his cow;
　　He climbed up a tree
　　And sat on a bough.
　　　He sat on a bough
　　　　And broke it in half,
　　　　　And John's old cow
　　　Did nothing but laugh.

ROSE FYLEMAN

LITTLE BOY BLUE

Little Boy Blue, come blow your horn;
The sheep's in the meadow, the cow's in the corn
Where's the little boy that looks after the sheep?
He's under the haystack, fast asleep.

LITTLE
MISS MUFFET

Little Miss Muffet
   Sat on a tuffet,
Eating of curds and whey;
   Along came a spider,
And sat down beside her,
   And frightened Miss Muffet away.

L

THREE
LITTLE
KITTENS

Three little kittens lost their mittens,
And they began to cry,
"Oh, mother dear,
We very much fear
That we have lost our mittens."

"Lost your mittens!
You naughty kittens!
Then you shall have no pie."
"Mee-ow, mee-ow, mee-ow."
"No, you shall have no pie."

The three little kittens found their mittens,
And they began to cry,
"Oh, mother dear,
See here, see here!
See, we have found our mittens."

"Put on your mittens,
You silly kittens,
And you shall have some pie."
"Purr-r, purr-r, purr-r.
Oh, let us have the pie!
Purr-r, purr-r, purr-r."

The three little kittens put on their mittens,
And soon ate up the pie.
"Oh, mother dear,
We greatly fear
That we have soiled our mittens!"

"Soiled your mittens!
You naughty kittens!"
Then they began to sigh,
"Mee-ow, mee-ow, mee-ow."
Then they began to sigh,
"Mee-ow, mee-ow, mee-ow."

The three little kittens washed their mittens,
And hung them up to dry.
"Oh, mother dear,
Do you not hear
That we have washed our mittens?"

"Washed your mittens!
Oh, you're good kittens,
But I smell a rat close by.

Hush! hush! Mee-ow, mee-ow."
"We smell a rat close by,
Mee-ow, mee-ow, mee-ow."

TO MARKET, TO MARKET

To market, to market,
To buy a fat pig,
Home again, home again,
Jiggety-jig.

To market, to market,
To buy a fat hog,
Home again, home again,
Jiggety-jog.

To market, to market,
To buy a plum bun,
Home again, home again,
Market is done.

HIGGLEDY, PIGGLEDY,
MY BLACK HEN

Higgledy, piggledy, my black hen,
She lays eggs for gentlemen;
Gentlemen come every day
To see what my black hen doth lay.

BAA, BAA, BLACK SHEEP

Baa, Baa, black sheep,
Have you any wool?
Yes sir, yes sir,
Three bags full:

One for my master,
And one for my dame,
And one for the little boy
Who lives in the lane.

LITTLE
ROBIN
REDBREAST

Little Robin Redbreast sat upon a tree;
Up went Pussycat, and down went he.
Down came Pussycat, and away Robin ran;
Said little Robin Redbreast, "Catch me if you can."

Little Robin Redbreast jumped upon a wall;
Pussycat jumped after him, and almost got a fall.
Little Robin chirped and sang, and what did Pussy say?
Pussycat said naught but "Mew," and Robin flew away.

ONCE I SAW A LITTLE BIRD

Once I saw a little bird
Come hop, hop, hop;
So I cried, "Little bird,
Will you stop, stop, stop?"
I was going to the window
To say, "How do you do?"
But he shook his little tail,
And far away he flew.

CHICK, CHICK, CHATTERMAN

Chick, chick, chatterman
  How much are your geese?
Chick, chick, chatterman
  Five cents apiece.
Chick, chick, chatterman
  That's too dear.
Chick, chick, chatterman
  Get out of here.

HEY, DIDDLE, DIDDLE

Hey, diddle, diddle!
  The cat and the fiddle,
The cow jumped over the moon;
  The little dog laughed
  To see such sport,
And the dish ran away with the spoon.

COCK-A-DOODLE-DOO

Cock-a-doodle-doo!
My dame has lost her shoe.
My master's lost his fiddling stick,
And doesn't know what to do!

Cock-a-doodle-doo!
What is my dame to do?
Till master finds his fiddling stick,
She'll dance without her shoe.

I HAD A COW

I had a cow that gave such milk
I dressed her in the finest silk;
I fed her on the finest hay,
And milked her twenty times a day.

TWO CATS OF KILKENNY

There once were two cats of Kilkenny,
Each thought there was one cat too many;
So they fought and they fit,
And they scratched and they bit,
Till, excepting their nails
And the tips of their tails,
Instead of two cats, there weren't any.

HIPPOPOTAMUS

Hi, hippopotamus, hip, hip, hip!
What an ugly face you've got,
what an ugly lip;
Can't you come and play a bit,
dance and hop and skip?
Come, hippopotamus, hip, hip, hip

ROSE FYLEMAN

36

SIMPLE SIMON

Simple Simon met a pieman,
  Going to the fair;
Says Simple Simon to the pieman,
  "Let me taste your ware."

Says the pieman unto Simon,
  "Show me first your penny."
Says Simple Simon to the pieman
  "Indeed, I have not any."

Simple Simon went a-fishing
  For to catch a whale;
All the water he could find
  Was in his mother's pail.

Simon went to catch a bird,
  And thought he could not fail,
Because he had a pinch of salt
  To put upon his tail.

I KNOW A MAN

I know a man named Michael Finnegan—
He wears whiskers on his chinnegan.
Along came a wind and blew them in again;
Poor old Michael Finnegan,
                                    begin again

BARBER, BARBER

Barber, barber, shave a pig;
How many hairs will make a wig?
"Four-and-twenty, that's enough."
Give the poor barber a pinch of snuff.

THERE WAS A
CROOKED MAN

There was a crooked man,
And he went a crooked mile,
He found a crooked sixpence,
Against a crooked stile;
He bought a crooked cat
Which caught a crooked mouse,
And they all lived together
In a little crooked house.

JACK SPRAT

Jack Sprat could eat no fat.
His wife could eat no lean;
And so betwixt the two of them,
They licked the platter clean.

OLD KING COLE

Old King Cole
Was a merry old soul,
And a merry old soul was he;
He called for his pipe,
He called for his bowl,
And he called for his fiddlers three.

Every fiddler, he had a fine fiddle
And a very fine fiddle had he;
Then twee, tweedle-dee,
Tweedle-dee went the fiddlers.
Oh, there's none so rare
As can compare
With King Cole and his fiddlers three!

THE
QUEEN
OF
HEARTS

The Queen of Hearts,
She made some tarts,
All on a summer's day.

The Knave of Hearts,
He stole those tarts,
And took them clean away.

The King of Hearts
Called for the tarts,
And beat the Knave full sore.

The Knave of Hearts
Brought back the tarts,
And vowed he'd steal no more.

SING A SONG OF SIXPENCE

Sing a song of sixpence,
    A pocket full of rye,
Four and twenty blackbirds
    Baked in a pie.
When the pie was opened,
    The birds began to sing.
Wasn't that a dainty dish
    To set before the King?

The King was in his counting house
    Counting out his money;
The Queen was in her parlor,
    Eating bread and honey;
The maid was in the garden,
    Hanging out the clothes,
Down came a blackbird
    And snapped off her nose.

POLLY, PUT THE KETTLE ON

Polly, put the kettle on,
Polly, put the kettle on,
Polly, put the kettle on,
We'll all have tea!

Sukey, take it off again,
Sukey, take it off again,
Sukey, take it off again,
They're all gone away.

TOMMY TUCKER

Little Tommy Tucker
Sings for his supper.
What shall he eat?
White bread and butter.

How shall he cut it
Without any knife?
How shall he marry
Without any wife?

HOT CROSS BUNS

Hot cross buns!
Hot cross buns!
One a penny, two a penny,
Hot cross buns!
If you have no daughters,
Give them to your sons.
One a penny, two a penny,
Hot cross buns!

Old Mother Hubbard

Old Mother Hubbard
Went to the cupboard,
To get her poor dog a bone;
But when she got there,
The cupboard was bare,
And so the poor dog had none.

She went to the baker's
To buy him some bread,
But when she came back,
The poor dog was dead.

She went to the fruiterer's
To buy him some fruit,
But when she came back,
He was playing the flute.

She went to the fishmonger's
To buy him some fish,
But when she came back,
He was licking the dish.

She went to the barber's
To buy him a wig,
But when she came back,
He was dancing a jig.

She went to the cobbler's
To buy him some shoes,
But when she came back,
He was reading the news.

She went to the tailor's
To buy him a coat,
But when she came back,
He was riding a goat.

The dame made a curtsy,
The dog made a bow;
The dame said, "Your servant,"
The dog said, "Bow-wow."

WIND IN THE EAST

When the wind is in the East,
'Tis neither good for man nor beast;
When the wind is in the North,
The skillful fisher goes not forth;
When the wind is in the South,
It blows the bait in the fishes' mouth;
When the wind is in the West,
Then 'tis at the very best.

DOCTOR FOSTER

Doctor Foster went to Gloucester,
In a shower of rain.
He stepped in a puddle,
Up to the middle,
And never went there again.

A SUNSHINY SHOWER

A sunshiny shower
Won't last an hour.

MARCH WINDS

March winds and April showers
Bring forth May flowers.

ONE MISTY, MOISTY MORNING

One misty, moisty morning,
When cloudy was the weather,
There I met an old man
Clothed all in leather.
He began to compliment
And I began to grin,
"How-do-you-do,"
And "how-do-you-do,"
And "how-do-you-do, again!"

THE
NORTH
WIND
DOTH
BLOW

The north wind doth blow,
  And we shall have snow,
And what will poor Robin do then, poor thing?
  He'll sit in a barn,
  To keep himself warm,
And hide his head under his wing, poor thing.

49

WEE WILLIE WINKIE

Wee Willie Winkie
　Runs through the town,
Upstairs and downstairs
　In his nightgown,
Rapping at the window,
　Crying through the lock,
"Are the children in their beds?
　For now it's eight o'clock."

HI-DI

Hi-di-doodledy-doo,
I think pink is better than blue;
I think fingers are better than thumbs,
I think stories are better than sums,
I think sand is better than sea;
Hi-di-doodledy-dee.

ROSE FYLEMAN

OLD CHAIRS TO MEND!

If I'd as much money a I could spend,
I never would cry old chairs to mend;
Old chairs to mend! Old chairs to mend!
I never would cry old chairs to mend.

DIDDLE, DIDDLE, DUMPLING

Diddle, diddle, dumpling, my son John,
He went to bed with his stockings on;
One shoe off, and one shoe on,
Diddle, diddle, dumpling, my son John.

GOOD NIGHT

The rabbits play no more,
   The little birds are weary,
The buttercups are folded up—
   Good night, good night, my dearie.

The children in the country,
   The children in the city
Go to their beds with nodding heads—
   Good night, good night, my pretty.

ROSE FYLEMAN

DOWN WITH THE LAMBS

Down with the lambs,
   Up with the lark,
Run to bed, children,
   Before it gets dark.

Poems
for
outdoors

FOUR SEASONS

Springtime is a green time
  When seedlings start their growing.
Summertime's a rainbow time
  When many blooms are blowing.
Autumntime's a brown time
  When seeds are ripe for sowing;
But wintertime's a white time
  (It is the flowers' nighttime)
When stars of frost are glowing.

ROWENA BASTIN BENNETT

THE WINTER IS PAST

For, lo, the winter is past,
  The rain is over and gone;
The flowers appear on the earth;
  The time of the singing of birds is come,
And the voice of the turtle is heard in our land.

THE SONG OF SOLOMON

54

SPRING WIND

The west wind dances down the lane
   and sets the robins winging;
It has a message sweet and plain,
   for some folks hear it singing:
O hurry, gather daffodils! They're scattered over all the hills
   As thick as anything!
The little buds unfold again, in buff and white and gold again—
   It's Spring, Spring, Spring!

The west wind races up the road
   and sets the green grass sprouting;
It wakes the turtle and the toad,
   and some folks hear it shouting:
O hurry, fetch your bat and ball, put on your oldest shoes of all,
   And cap and everything.
It's turning fine and hot again, the boys are in the lot again—
   It's Spring, Spring, Spring!

NANCY BYRD TURNER

SPRING MORNING

Where am I going? I don't quite know.
Down to the stream where the king-cups grow—
Up on the hill where the pine trees blow—
Anywhere, anywhere. *I* don't know.

Where am I going? The clouds sail by,
Little ones, baby ones, over the sky.
Where am I going? The shadows pass,
Little ones, baby ones, over the grass.

If you were a cloud, and sailed up there,
You'd sail on water as blue as air,
And you'd see me here in the fields and say:
"Doesn't the sky look green today?"

Where am I going? The high rooks call:
"It's awful fun to be born at all."
Where am I going? The ring-doves coo:
"We do have beautiful things to do."

If you were a bird, and lived on high,
You'd lean on the wind when the wind came by,
You'd say to the wind when it took you away:
"*That's* where I wanted to go today!"

Where am I going? I don't quite know.
What does it matter where people go?
Down to the wood where the bluebells grow—
Anywhere, anywhere. *I* don't know.

A. A. MILNE

THE YEAR'S AT THE SPRING

The year's at the spring
And the day's at the morn;
Morning's at seven;
The hillside's dew-pearled;
The lark's on the wing;
The snail's on the thorn:
God's in his Heaven—
All's right with the world!

ROBERT BROWNING

BAREFOOT
DAYS

In the morning, very early,
That's the time I love to go
Barefoot where the fern grows curly
And grass is cool between each toe,
On a summer morning—O!
On a summer morning!

That is when the birds go by
Up the sunny slopes of air,
And each rose has a butterfly
Or a golden bee to wear;
And I am glad in every toe—
Such a summer morning—O!
Such a summer morning!

RACHEL FIELD

58

A SUMMER MORNING

I saw dawn creep across the sky,
And all the gulls go flying by.
I saw the sea put on its dress
Of blue midsummer loveliness,
And heard the trees begin to stir
Green arms of pine and juniper.
I heard the wind call out and say:
"Get up, my dear, it is today!"

RACHEL FIELD

SUMMER EVENING

The sandy cat by the Farmer's chair
Mews at his knee for dainty fare;
Old Rover in his moss-greened house
Mumbles a bone, and barks at a mouse.
In the dewy fields the cattle lie
Chewing the cud 'neath a fading sky;
Dobbin at manger pulls his hay:
Gone is another summer's day.

WALTER DE LA MARE

BED IN SUMMER

In winter I get up at night
And dress by yellow candlelight.
In summer, quite the other way,
I have to go to bed by day.

I have to go to bed and see
The birds still hopping on the tree,
Or hear the grown-up people's feet
Still going past me in the street.

And does it not seem hard to you,
When all the sky is clear and blue,
And I should like so much to play,
To have to go to bed by day?

ROBERT LOUIS STEVENSON

AUTUMN FIRES

In the other gardens
  And all up the vale,
From the autumn bonfires
  See the smoke trail!

Pleasant summer over
  And all the summer flowers,
The red fire blazes,
  The gray smoke towers.

Sing a song of seasons!
  Something bright in all!
Flowers in the summer,
  Fires in the fall!

ROBERT LOUIS STEVENSON

AUTUMN

The morns are meeker than they were,
  The nuts are getting brown;
The berry's cheek is plumper,
  The rose is out of town.
The maple wears a gayer scarf,
  The field a scarlet gown.
Lest I should be old-fashioned,
  I'll put a trinket on.

EMILY DICKINSON

A VAGABOND SONG

There is something in the Autumn
      that is native to my blood—
Touch of manner, hint of mood;
And my heart is like a rhyme,
With the yellow and the purple
      and the crimson keeping time.
The scarlet of the maples
      can shake me like a cry
Of bugles going by.
And my lonely spirit thrills
To see the frosty asters
      like smoke upon the hills.
There is something in October
      sets the gypsy blood astir,
We must rise and follow her,
When from every hill of flame
She calls and calls each vagabond by name.

BLISS CARMAN

THE MIST AND ALL

I like the fall,
The mist and all.
I like the night owl's
Lonely call—
And wailing sound
Of wind around.

I like the gray
November day,
And bare dead boughs
That coldly sway
Against my pane.
I like the rain.

I like to sit
And laugh at it—
And tend
My cozy fire a bit.
I like the fall—
The mist and all.

DIXIE WILLSON

AUTUMN SONG

These are the days of falling leaves,
The days of hazy weather,
Smelling of gold chrysanthemums
And gray wood smoke together.

These are the nights of nearby stars,
The nights of closer moons,
When the windy darkness echoes
To crickets' farewell tunes.

ELIZABETH-ELLEN LONG

WINTER

The street cars are
Like frosted cakes—
All covered up
With cold snowflakes.

The horses' hoofs
Scrunch on the street;
Their eyelashes
Are white with sleet.

And everywhere
The people go
With faces *tickled*
By the snow.

DOROTHY ALDIS

THE SNOWBIRD

When all the ground with snow is white,
    The merry snowbird comes,
And hops about with great delight
    To find the scattered crumbs.

How glad he seems to get to eat
    A piece of cake or bread!
He wears no shoes upon his feet,
    Nor hat upon his head.

But happiest is he, I know,
    Because no cage with bars
Keeps him from walking on the snow
    And printing it with stars.

FRANK DEMPSTER SHERMAN

COLD WINTER

Cold winter now is in the wood,
The moon wades deep in snow.
Pile balsam boughs about the sills,
And let the fires glow!

The cows must stand in the dark barn,
The horses stamp all day.
Now shall the housewife bake her pies
And keep her kitchen gay.

The cat sleeps warm beneath the stove,
The dog on paws outspread;
But the brown deer with flinching hide
Seeks for a sheltered bed.

The fox steps hungry through the brush,
The lean hawk coasts the sky.
"Winter is in the wood!" the winds
In the warm chimney cry.

ELIZABETH COATSWORTH

WHITE FIELDS

In the wintertime we go
Walking in the fields of snow;

Where there is no grass at all;
Where the top of every wall,

Every fence and every tree,
Is as white as white can be.

Pointing out the way we came,
—Every one of them the same—

All across the fields there be
Prints in silver filigree;

And our mothers always know,
By the footprints in the snow,

Where it is the children go.

JAMES STEPHENS

FEBRUARY TWILIGHT

I stood beside a hill
   Smooth with new-laid snow,
A single star looked out
   From the cold evening glow.

There was no other creature
   That saw what I could see—
I stood and watched the evening star
   As long as it watched me.

SARA TEASDALE

THE
DAY
BEFORE
APRIL

The day before April
Alone, alone,
I walked in the woods
And sat on a stone.

I sat on a broad stone
And sang to the birds.
The tune was God's making
But I made the words.

MARY CAROLYN DAVIES

MARCH

Dear March, come in!
How glad I am!
I looked for you before.
Put down your hat—
You must have walked—
How out of breath you are!
Dear March, how are you?
And the rest?
Did you leave Nature well?
Oh, March,
   come right upstairs with me,
I have so much to tell!

EMILY DICKINSON

APRIL

The roofs are shining from the rain,
   The sparrows twitter as they fly,
And with a windy April grace
   The little clouds go by.

Yet the back yards are bare and brown
   With only one unchanging tree—
I could not be so sure of Spring
   Save that it sings in me.

SARA TEASDALE

MAY MORNINGS

May mornings are merry,
May mornings are gay,
For every green hedgerow
Is fragrant with may,
And every blithe blackbird
Is singing like mad,
And nothing is dreary
Or weary or sad.
The sun's warm and friendly,
The breeze soft and cool,
And gay little children
Go dancing to school.

IVY O. EASTWICK

JULY

When the scarlet cardinal tells
  Her dream to the dragonfly,
And the lazy breeze makes a nest in the trees,
  And murmurs a lullaby,
    It is July.

When the tangled cobweb pulls
  The cornflower's cap awry,
And the lilies tall lean over the wall
  To bow to the butterfly,
    It is July.

When the heat like a mist veil floats,
  And poppies flame in the rye,
And the silver note in the streamlet's throat
  Has softened almost to a sigh,
    It is July.

When the hours are so still that time
  Forgets them, and lets them lie
'Neath petals pink till the night stars wink
  At the sunset in the sky,
    It is July.

SUSAN HARTLEY SWETT

IN AUGUST

When the sun is strong
And the day is hot,
We move around
At a peaceful trot.
We don't wear much
In the way of clothes
And we squirt ourselves
With the garden hose.

MARCHETTE CHUTE

GLIMPSE IN AUTUMN

Ladies at a ball
    Are not so fine as these
Richly brocaded trees
    That decorate the fall.

They stand against a wall
    Of crisp October sky,
Their plumèd heads held high,
    Like ladies at a ball.

JEAN STARR UNTERMEYER

SEPTEMBER

A road like brown ribbon,
    A sky that is blue,
A forest of green
    With that sky peeping through.

Asters, deep purple,
    A grasshopper's call,
Today it is summer,
    Tomorrow is fall.

EDWINA FALLIS

OCTOBER

The summer is over,
    The trees are all bare,
There is mist in the garden
    And frost in the air.
The meadows are empty
    And gathered the sheaves—
But isn't it lovely
    Kicking up leaves!

John from the garden
    Has taken the chairs;
It's dark in the evening
    And cold on the stairs.
Winter is coming
    And everyone grieves—
But isn't it lovely
    Kicking up leaves!

ROSE FYLEMAN

NOVEMBER

November comes,
And November goes
With the last red berries
And the first white snows,

With night coming early
And dawn coming late,
And ice in the bucket
And frost by the gate.

The fires burn
And the kettles sing,
And earth sinks to rest
Until next spring.

ELIZABETH COATSWORTH

DECEMBER

I like days
with a snow-white collar,
and nights when the moon
is a silver dollar,
and hills are filled
with eiderdown stuffing
and your breath makes smoke
like an engine puffing.

I like days
when feathers are snowing,
and all the eaves
have petticoats showing,
and the air is cold,
and the wires are humming,
but you feel all warm . . .
with Christmas coming!

AILEEN FISHER

CHECK

The Night was creeping on the ground!
She crept and did not make a sound,

Until she reached the tree: And then
She covered it, and stole again

Along the grass beside the wall!
—I heard the rustling of her shawl

As she threw blackness everywhere
Along the sky, the ground, the air,

And in the room where I was hid!
But, no matter what she did

To everything that was without,
She could not put my candle out!

So I stared at the Night! And she
Stared back solemnly at me!

JAMES STEPHENS

MOON SONG

There is a star that runs very fast,
That goes pulling the moon
Through the tops of the poplars.
It is all in silver,
The tall star:
The moon rolls goldenly along
Out of breath—
Mr. Moon, does he make you hurry?

HILDA CONKLING

THIS IS MY ROCK

This is my rock
And here I run
To steal the secret of the sun;

This is my rock
And here come I
Before the night has swept the sky;

This is my rock,
This is the place
I meet the evening face to face.

DAVID MC CORD

THE MOON'S THE NORTH WIND'S COOKY

(What the Little Girl said)

The Moon's the North Wind's cooky.
He bites it, day by day,
Until there's but a rim of scraps
That crumble all away.

The South Wind is a baker.
He kneads clouds in his den.
And bakes a crisp new moon *that—greedy
North—Wind—eats—again!*

VACHEL LINDSAY

THE FALLING STAR

I saw a star slide down the sky,
Blinding the north as it went by,
Too burning and too quick to hold,
Too lovely to be bought or sold,
Good only to make wishes on
And then forever to be gone.

76   SARA TEASDALE

STARS

Bright stars, light stars,
Shining-in-the-night stars,
Little twinkly, winkly stars,
Deep in the sky!

Yellow stars, red stars,
Shine-when-I'm-in-bed stars,
Oh how many blinky stars,
Far, far away!

RHODA W. BACMEISTER

TWINKLE, TWINKLE, LITTLE STAR

Twinkle, twinkle, little star,
How I wonder what you are!
Up above the world so high,
Like a diamond in the sky.

JANE TAYLOR

NIGHT

My kitten walks on velvet feet
And makes no sound at all;
And in the doorway nightly sits
To watch the darkness fall.

I think he loves the lady, Night,
And feels akin to her
Whose footsteps are as still as his,
Whose touch as soft as fur.

LOIS WEAKLEY MCKAY

77

SUNRISE

I've never seen the great sun rise,
For then I am in bed;
The sands of slumber in my eyes
Hold down my drowsy head.

I *think* the sun climbs up the sky
And throws the clouds away,
Then girds her flaming tunic high
And strides to meet the day.

Soft-touched by birds' wings is her head;
Her feet caressed by trees;
She turns their leaves to gold and red
And stoops to drink the seas.

KATHARINE KOSMAK

THE SUN

I told the Sun that I was glad,
I'm sure I don't know why;
Somehow the pleasant way he had
Of shining in the sky
Just put a notion in my head
That wouldn't it be fun
If, walking on the hill, I said
"I'm happy" to the Sun.

JOHN DRINKWATER

SONG OF THE WAKE-UP-WORLD

Wake up, O World; O World, awake!
The light is bright on hill and lake;
O World, awake; wake up, O World!
The flags of the wind are all unfurled;
Wake up, O World; O World, awake!
Of earth's delightfulness partake.

Wake up, O World, whatever hour;
Sweet are the fields, sweet is the flower!
Wake up, O World; O World, awake;
Perhaps to see the daylight break,
Perhaps to see the sun descend,
The night begin, the daylight end.

But something surely to behold,
Not bought with silver or with gold,
Not shown in any land of dreams.
For open eyes the whole world teems
With lovely things to do or make,
Wake up, O World; O World, awake!

COUNTEE CULLEN

MORNING

Will there really be a morning?
    Is there such a thing as day?
Could I see it from the mountains
    If I were as tall as they?
Has it feet like water lilies?
    Has it feathers like a bird?
Is it brought from famous countries
    Of which I've never heard?
Oh, some scholar! Oh, some sailor!
    Oh, some wise man from the skies!
Please to tell a little pilgrim
    Where the place called *morning* lies!

EMILY DICKINSON

AFTERNOON ON A HILL

I will be the gladdest thing
    Under the sun!
I will touch a hundred flowers
    And not pick one.

I will look at cliffs and clouds
    With quiet eyes,
Watch the wind bow down the grass,
    And the grass rise.

And when lights begin to show
    Up from the town,
I will mark which must be mine,
    And then start down!

EDNA ST. VINCENT MILLAY

81

MY SHADOW

I have a little shadow that goes in and out with me,
And what can be the use of him is more than I can see.
He is very, very like me from the heels up to the head;
And I see him jump before me, when I jump into my bed.

The funniest thing about him is the way he likes to grow—
Not at all like proper children, which is always very slow;
For he sometimes shoots up taller like an India-rubber ball,
And he sometimes gets so little that there's none of him at all.

He hasn't got a notion of how children ought to play,
And can only make a fool of me in every sort of way.
He stays so close beside me, he's a coward you can see;
I'd think shame to stick to nursie as that shadow sticks to me!

One morning, very early, before the sun was up,
I rose and found the shining dew on every buttercup;
But my lazy little shadow, like an arrant sleepyhead,
Had stayed at home behind me and was fast asleep in bed.

ROBERT LOUIS STEVENSON

SHADOW DANCE

O Shadow,
Dear Shadow,
Come, Shadow,
And dance!
On the wall
In the firelight
Let both of
Us prance!
I raise my
Arms, thus!
And you raise
Your arms, so!
And dancing
And leaping
And laughing
We go!
From the wall
To the ceiling,
From ceiling
To wall,
Just you and
I, Shadow,
And none else
At all.

IVY O. EASTWICK

THE WIND

I saw you toss the kites on high
And blow the birds about the sky;
And all around I heard you pass,
Like ladies' skirts across the grass—
    O wind, a-blowing all day long,
    O wind, that sings so loud a song!

I saw the different things you did,
But always you yourself you hid.
I felt you push, I heard you call,
I could not see yourself at all—
    O wind, a-blowing all day long,
    O wind, that sings so loud a song!

O you that are so strong and cold,
O blower, are you young or old?
Are you a beast of field and tree,
Or just a stronger child than me?
    O wind, a-blowing all day long,
    O wind, that sings so loud a song!

ROBERT LOUIS STEVENSON

WHO HAS SEEN THE WIND?

Who has seen the wind?
  Neither I nor you;
But when the leaves hang trembling,
  The wind is passing through.

Who has seen the wind?
  Neither you nor I;
But when the trees
  Bow down their heads,
The wind is passing by.

CHRISTINA ROSSETTI

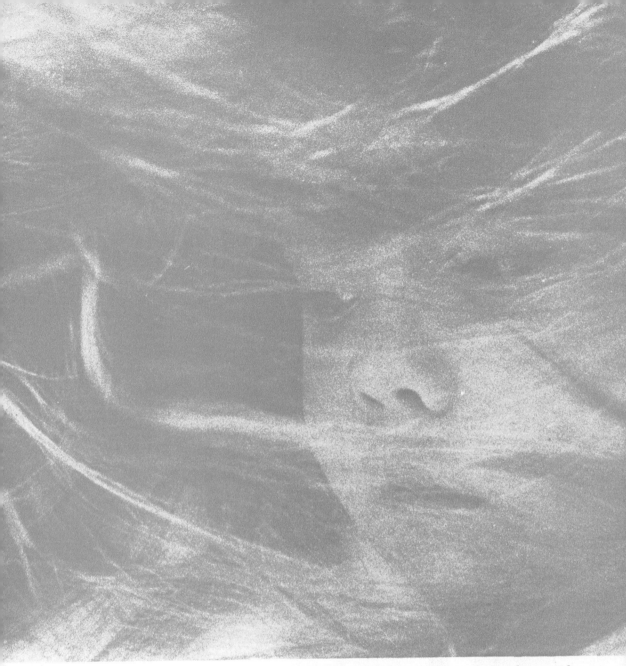

WIND CAPERS

The wind is out with a leap and a twirl,
  Prancing, prancing,
The aspen tree is like a girl,
  Dancing, dancing.
The maple tree upon the hill,
  She cannot keep her ruffles still.
The swallows blow along the sky,
  Glancing, glancing,
O wind, O wind, you tricky elf,
  Behave yourself!

NANCY BYRD TURNER

85

CLOUDS

White sheep, white sheep,
On a blue hill,
When the wind stops
You all stand still.
When the wind blows
You walk away slow.
White sheep, white sheep,
Where do you go?

CHRISTINA ROSSETTI

WINDS A-BLOWING

The North Wind is a beggar
Who shudders at the cold.
The South Wind is a sailor
With pockets full of gold.
The East Wind is a gypsy
With saucy cap and feather.
The West Wind is a wizard
Who conjures wicked weather.

The Winter Wind's a giant
As grumpy as a bear.
The Summer Wind's a lady
With flowers in her hair.
The Autumn Wind's an old man
As touchy as a thistle.
The Spring Wind is a gay lad
Who blows a silver whistle.

MAY JUSTUS

BROOMS

On stormy days
When the wind is high
Tall trees are brooms
Sweeping the sky.

They swish their branches
In buckets of rain,
And swash and sweep it
Blue again.

DOROTHY ALDIS

GARMENT

The clouds weave a shawl
Of downy plaid
For the sky to put on
When the weather's bad.

LANGSTON HUGHES

87

Rain, Rain, Go Away

Rain, rain, go away,
Come again another day;
Little Johnny wants to play.

OLD RHYME

DOWN THE RAIN FALLS

Down the rain falls,
Up crackles the fire,
Tick-tock goes the clock
Neither lower nor higher—

Such soft little sounds
As sleepy hens make
When they talk to themselves
For company's sake.

ELIZABETH COATSWORTH

RAIN

The rain is raining all around,
It falls on field and tree,
It rains on the umbrellas here,
And on the ships at sea.

ROBERT LOUIS STEVENSON

"Pitter patter!" falls the rain
On the schoolroom windowpane.
Such a plashing! such a dashing!
Will it e'er be dry again?
Down the gutter rolls a flood,
And the crossing's deep in mud;
And the puddles! oh, the puddles
Are a sight to stir one's blood!

THE UMBRELLA BRIGADE

Chorus.

But let it rain
Tree toads and frogs,
Muskets and pitchforks,
Kittens and dogs!
Dash away! plash away!
Who is afraid?
Here we go,
The Umbrella Brigade!

Pull the boots up to the knee!
Tie the hoods on merrily!
Such a hustling! such a jostling!
Out of breath with fun are we.
Clatter, clatter, down the street,
Greeting every one we meet,
With our laughing and our chaffing,
Which the laughing drops repeat.

Chorus.

So let it rain
Tree toads and frogs,
Muskets and pitchforks,
Kittens and dogs!
Dash away! plash away!
Who is afraid?
Here we go,
The Umbrella Brigade!

LAURA E. RICHARDS

RAIN IN THE NIGHT

Raining, raining,
All night long;
Sometimes loud, sometimes soft,
Just like a song.

There'll be rivers in the gutters
And lakes along the street.
It will make our lazy kitty
Wash his little dirty feet.

The roses will wear diamonds
Like kings and queens at court;
But the pansies all get muddy
Because they are so short.

I'll sail my boat tomorrow
In wonderful new places,
But first I'll take my watering pot
And wash the pansies' faces.

AMELIA JOSEPHINE BURR

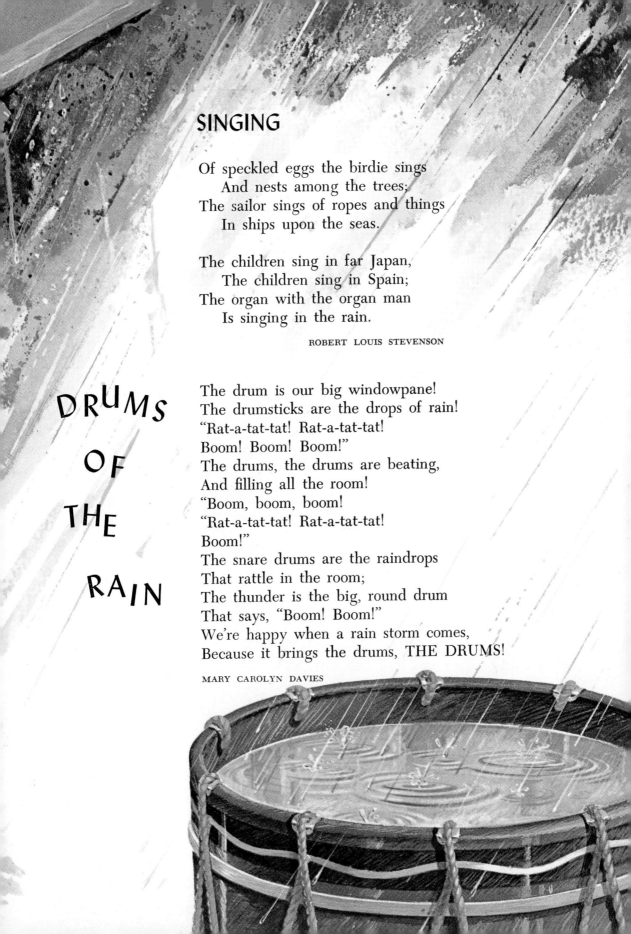

SINGING

Of speckled eggs the birdie sings
    And nests among the trees;
The sailor sings of ropes and things
    In ships upon the seas.

The children sing in far Japan,
    The children sing in Spain;
The organ with the organ man
    Is singing in the rain.

ROBERT LOUIS STEVENSON

DRUMS OF THE RAIN

The drum is our big windowpane!
The drumsticks are the drops of rain!
"Rat-a-tat-tat! Rat-a-tat-tat!
Boom! Boom! Boom!"
The drums, the drums are beating,
And filling all the room!
"Boom, boom, boom!
"Rat-a-tat-tat! Rat-a-tat-tat!
Boom!"
The snare drums are the raindrops
That rattle in the room;
The thunder is the big, round drum
That says, "Boom! Boom!"
We're happy when a rain storm comes,
Because it brings the drums, THE DRUMS!

MARY CAROLYN DAVIES

IN TIME OF SILVER RAIN

In time of silver rain
The butterflies lift silken wings
To catch a rainbow cry,
And trees put forth
New leaves to sing
In joy beneath the sky
As down the roadway passing boys
And girls go singing, too,
In time of silver rain
When spring
And life are new.

LANGSTON HUGHES

THE RAINBOW

Boats sail on the rivers,
  And ships sail on the seas;
But clouds that sail across the sky
  Are prettier far than these.

There are bridges on the rivers,
  As pretty as you please;
But the bow that bridges heaven,
  And overtops the trees,
And builds a road from earth to sky,
  Is prettier far than these.

CHRISTINA ROSSETTI

JACKY FROST

Jacky Frost, Jacky Frost,
  Came in the night;
Left the meadows that he crossed
  All gleaming white.
Painted with his silver brush
  Every windowpane;
Kissed the leaves and made them blush,
  Blush and blush again.

Jacky Frost, Jacky Frost,
  Crept around the house,
Sly as a silver fox,
  Still as a mouse.
Out little Jenny came,
  Blushing like a rose;
Up jumped Jacky Frost,
  And pinched her little nose.

LAURA E. RICHARDS

LOOK AT THE SNOW!

Look at the snow!
  Look at the snow!
Let's all take our sleds,
  And go!
Up the hill we walk slow, slow,
And drag our red sleds in the snow;
But once at the top of the hill, we know
That like the wind they'll go, go, go,
Whizzing down to the flat, below.
Oh, the fun as we swiftly fly
Over the snow like a bird on high!
It takes our breath as our sleds speed by;
No one's as happy as you and I!
—Summers may come, and summers may go,
But *we* like the snow, the snow, the snow!

MARY CAROLYN DAVIES

SLIDING

We can slide
        down
            the
                hill
or
      down
         the
             street
or anywhere.
Or down the roof
      where the shingles broke,
Or down the trunk
      of the back-yard oak.

Down
  the
    slide
        or the ice
        or the slippery street,

We can slide on our sled
       or our skates
       or our feet.
Oh, it's lots of fun to go outside
And slide
    and slide
      and slide
        and slide.

MYRA COHN

SLEET STORM

TIC-TIC-TIC!
The sound of the sleet
Fell like the beat
Of tiny feet,
Racing and chasing down the street:
The quick sharp beat
Of a million hoofs
Clicked and clattered
Across the roofs.
The sleet storm fell
Through a day and a night
With a tic-tic-tic
That was fast and light.

On the second morning
A cold sun shone
On a glittering, crystal,
Frigid zone.
Each bush and branch
Was icily hung
With the frozen song
The sleet had sung.
The branches swayed
With their icy load
Where millions of diamonds
Flashed and glowed.
Steep roofs shone
With a blinding glare,
Fringed with icicles
Everywhere.
But the tic-tic-tic
Of the sleet was still,
Caught on each glistening
Valley and hill.

JAMES S. TIPPETT

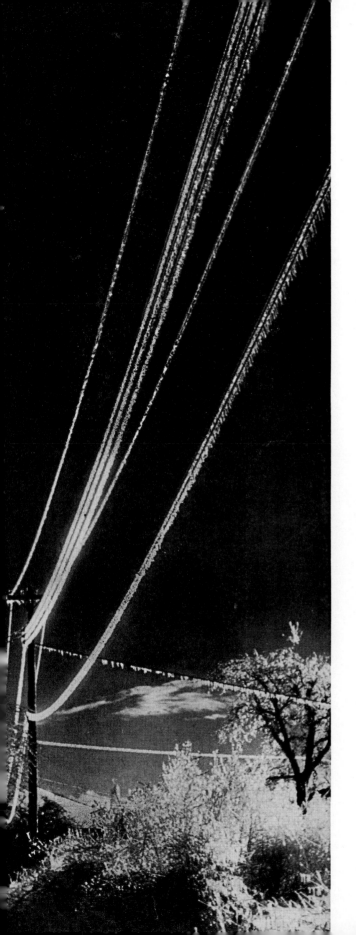

ICE

When it is the winter time
   I run up the street
And I make the ice laugh
   With my little feet—
"Crickle, crackle, crickle
   Crrreeet, crrreeet, crrreeet."

DOROTHY ALDIS

THAW

The snow is soft,
   and how it squashes!
"Galumph, galumph!"
   go my galoshes.

EUNICE TIETJENS

FOG

The fog comes
on little cat feet.
It sits looking
over harbor and city
on silent haunches
and then moves on.

CARL SANDBURG

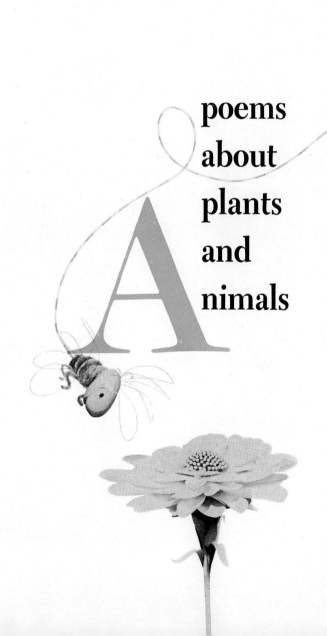

poems
about
plants
and
nimals

VOL. I

LIVING
ANIMALS
OF THE
WORLD

A KITTEN

He's nothing much but fur
And two round eyes of blue,
He has a giant purr
And a midget mew.

He darts and pats the air,
He starts and cocks his ear,
When there is nothing there
For him to see and hear.

He runs around in rings,
But why we cannot tell;
With sideways leaps he springs
At things invisible—

Then halfway through a leap
His startled eyeballs close,
And he drops off to sleep
With one paw on his nose.

ELEANOR FARJEON

LITTLE PUSSY

I like little Pussy,
Her coat is so warm;
And if I don't hurt her,
She'll do me no harm.

So I'll not pull her tail,
Nor drive her away,
But Pussy and I
Very gently will play.

JANE TAYLOR

DOGS AND WEATHER

I'd like a different dog
    For every kind of weather—
A narrow greyhound for a fog,
    A wolfhound strange and white,
With a tail like a silver feather
    To run with in the night,
When snow is still, and winter stars are bright.

In the fall I'd like to see
    In answer to my whistle,
A golden spaniel look at me.
    But best of all for rain
A terrier, hairy as a thistle,
    To trot with fine disdain
Beside me down the soaked, sweet-smelling lane.

WINIFRED WELLES

DOGS

The dogs I know
Have many shapes.
For some are big and tall,
And some are long,
And some are thin,
And some are fat and small.
And some are little bits of fluff
And have no shape at all.

MARCHETTE CHUTE

HOLDING
HANDS

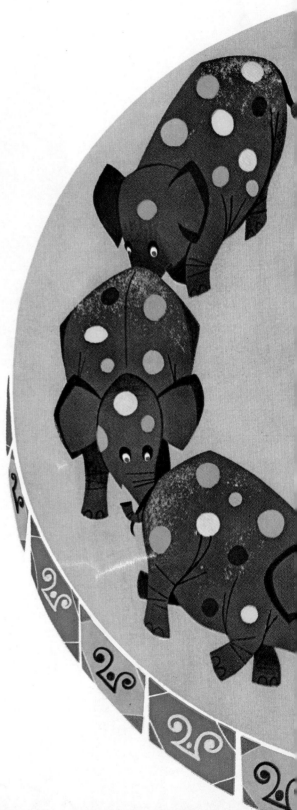

Elephants walking
Along the trails

Are holding hands
By holding tails.

Trunks and tails
Are handy things

When elephants walk
In circus rings.

Elephants work
And elephants play

And elephants walk
And feel so gay.

And when they walk—
It never fails

They're holding hands
By holding tails.

106   LENORE M. LINK

THE ELEPHANT

When people call this beast to mind,
They marvel more and more
At such a *little* tail behind,
So LARGE a trunk before.

HILAIRE BELLOC

107

WHISKY
FRISKY

WHISKY Frisky,
Hippity-hop
Up he goes
To the treetop!

Whirly, twirly,
Round and round,
Down he scampers
To the ground.

Furly, curly,
What a tail!
Tall as a feather,
Broad as a sail!

Where's his supper?
In the shell,
Snap, cracky,
Out it fell.

AUTHOR UNKNOWN

THE REASON

Rabbits and squirrels
Are furry and fat,
And all of the chickens
Have feathers, and *that*
Is why when it's raining
They need not stay in
The way children do who have
Only their skin.

DOROTHY ALDIS

THE RABBIT

When they said the time to hide was mine,
I hid back under a thick grapevine.

And while I was still for the time to pass,
A little gray thing came out of the grass.

He hopped his way through the melon bed
And sat down close by a cabbage head.

He sat down close where I could see,
And his big still eyes looked hard at me,

His big eyes bursting out of the rim,
And I looked back very hard at him.

ELIZABETH MADOX ROBERTS

FURRY BEAR

If I were a bear,
  And a big bear too,
I shouldn't much care
  If it froze or snew;
I shouldn't much mind
  If it snowed or friz—
I'd be all fur-lined
  With a coat like his!

For I'd have fur boots and a brown fur wrap,
And brown fur knickers and a big fur cap.
I'd have a fur muffle-ruff to cover my jaws,
And brown fur mittens on my big brown paws.
With a big brown furry-down up to my head,
I'd sleep all the winter in a big fur bed.

A. A. MILNE

BABY GOAT

Did you ever pat a baby goat
And learn how soft he feels?
Did you ever watch him walk about
On his four little black high heels?

ZHENYA GAY

It is a curious thing that you
don't wish to be a kangaroo,
to hop hop hop
and never stop
the whole day long and the whole night, too!

to hop across Australian plains
with tails that sweep behind like trains
and small front paws
and pointed jaws
and pale neat coats to shed the rains.

THE KANGAROO

If skies be blue, if skies be gray,
they bound in the same graceful way
into dim space
at such a pace
that where they go there's none to say!

ELIZABETH COATSWORTH

BIGGER

The cow is big. Her eyes are round.
She makes a very scary sound.

I'm rather glad the fence is tall—
I don't feel quite so weak and small.

And yet I'm not afraid. You see,
I'm six years old—and she's just three.

DOROTHY BROWN THOMPSON

THE COW

The friendly cow all red and white,
I love with all my heart:
She gives me cream with all her might,
To eat with apple tart.

She wanders lowing here and there,
And yet she cannot stray,
All in the pleasant open air,
The pleasant light of day;

And blown by all the winds that pass
And wet with all the showers,
She walks among the meadow grass
And eats the meadow flowers.

ROBERT LOUIS STEVENSON

HORSES

Back and forth
and up and down,
horses' tails go switching.

Up and down
and back and forth,
horses' skins go twitching.

Horses do
a lot of work
to keep themselves from itching.

AILEEN FISHER

jump or jiggle

Frogs jump
Caterpillars hump

Worms wiggle
Bugs jiggle

Rabbits hop
Horses clop

Snakes slide
Sea gulls glide

Mice creep
Deer leap

Puppies bounce
Kittens pounce

Lions stalk—
But—
I walk!

EVELYN BEYER

the little turtle

There was a little turtle.
He lived in a box.
He swam in a puddle.
He climbed on the rocks.

He snapped at a mosquito,
He snapped at a flea,
He snapped at a minnow.
And he snapped at me.

He caught the mosquito,
He caught the flea,
He caught the minnow.
But he didn't catch me.

VACHEL LINDSAY

snail

Little snail,
Dreaming you go.
Weather and rose
Is all you know.

Weather and rose
Is all you see,
Drinking
The dewdrop's
Mystery.

LANGSTON HUGHES

LITTLE BLACK BUG

Little black bug,
Little black bug,
Where have you been?
I've been under the rug,
Said little black bug.
Bug-ug-ug-ug.

Little green fly,
Little green fly,
Where have you been?
I've been way up high,
Said little green fly.
Bzzzzzzzzzzzzzz.

Little old mouse,
Little old mouse,
Where have you been?
I've been all through the house,
Said little old mouse.
Squeak-eak-eak-eak-eak.

MARGARET WISE BROWN

FUZZY WUZZY,
CREEPY CRAWLY

Fuzzy wuzzy, creepy crawly
        Caterpillar funny,
You will be a butterfly
When the days are sunny.

Winging, flinging, dancing, springing
        Butterfly so yellow,
You were once a caterpillar,
        Wiggly, wiggly fellow.

LILLIAN SCHULZ

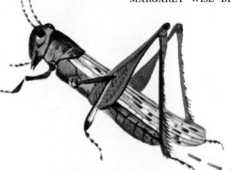

AN EXPLANATION OF
THE GRASSHOPPER

THE Grasshopper, the Grasshopper,
I will explain to you:—
He is the Brownies' racehorse,
The Fairies' Kangaroo.

VACHEL LINDSAY

THE CATERPILLAR

Brown and furry
Caterpillar in a hurry
Take your walk
To the shady leaf, or stalk,
Or what not,
Which may be the chosen spot.
No toad spy you,
Hovering bird of prey pass by you;
Spin and die,
To live again a butterfly.

CHRISTINA ROSSETTI

THE CRICKET

And when the rain had gone away
And it was shining everywhere,
I ran out on the walk to play
And found a little bug was there.

And he was running just as fast
As any little bug could run,
Until he stopped for breath at last,
All black and shiny in the sun.

And then he chirped a song to me
And gave his wings a little tug,
And *that's* the way he showed that he
Was very glad to be a bug!

MARJORIE BARROWS

TO A FIREFLY

Stars are twinkling up on high,
Moon hangs low in eastern sky;
These with thee do not compare,
Cheerful beacon of the air—

Speeding onward through the dark,
Beneath the oak trees in the park,
With thy glowing, gleaming light,
Happy lightning bug of night.

J. MORRIS JONES

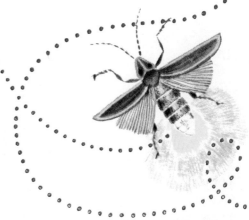

FIREFLY (A *song*)

A little light is going by,
Is going up to see the sky,
A little light with wings.

I never could have thought of it,
To have a little bug all lit
And made to go on wings.

ELIZABETH MADOX ROBERTS

WHO IS SO PRETTY?

Skitter, skatter,
Leap and squeak!
We've been dancing
Half the week.

Under the sofa,
Along the shelf,
Every mouse
Is wild as an elf.

Big round ear
And bright black eye,
Nimble and natty,
Limber and spry—

Who is so pretty,
Who is so neat,
As a little mouse dancing
On little gray feet?

ELIZABETH COATSWORTH

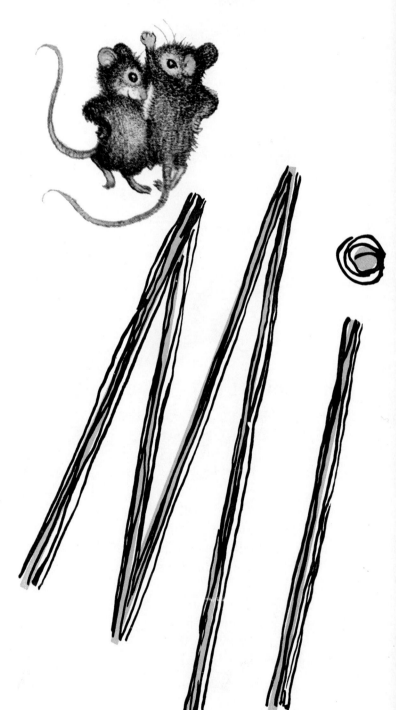

MICE

I think mice
Are rather nice.

Their tails are long,
Their faces small,
They haven't any
Chins at all.
Their ears are pink,
Their teeth are white,
They run about
The house at night.
They nibble things
They shouldn't touch
And no one seems
To like them much.

But *I* think mice
Are nice.

ROSE FYLEMAN

THE HOUSE
OF THE MOUSE

The house of the mouse
is a wee little house,
a green little house in the grass,
which big clumsy folk
may hunt and may poke
and still never see as they pass
this sweet little, neat little,
wee little, green little,
cuddle-down hide-away
house in the grass.

LUCY SPRAGUE MITCHELL

THE CITY MOUSE
AND THE GARDEN MOUSE

The city mouse lives in a house;
The garden mouse lives in a bower,
He's friendly with the frogs and toads,
And sees the pretty plants in flower.

The city mouse eats bread and cheese;
The garden mouse eats what he can;
We will not grudge him seeds and stalks,
Poor little timid furry man.

CHRISTINA ROSSETTI

MOUSE

Little Mouse in gray velvet,
Have you had a cheese breakfast?
There are no crumbs on your coat,
Did you use a napkin?
I wonder what you had to eat,
And who dresses you in gray velvet?

HILDA CONKLING

SOMETHING TOLD THE WILD GEESE

Something told the wild geese
It was time to go.
Though the fields lay golden
Something whispered, "Snow."
Leaves were green and stirring,
Berries, luster-glossed,
But beneath warm feathers
Something cautioned, "Frost."
All the sagging orchards
Steamed with amber spice,
But each wild breast stiffened
At remembered ice.
Something told the wild geese
It was time to fly—
Summer sun was on their wings,
Winter in their cry.

RACHEL FIELD

THE WOODPECKER

The woodpecker pecked out a little round hole
And made him a house in the telephone pole.
One day when I watched he poked out his head,
And he had on a hood and a collar of red.

When the streams of rain pour out of the sky,
And the sparkles of lightning go flashing by,
And the big, big wheels of thunder roll,
He can snuggle back in the telephone pole.

ELIZABETH MADOX ROBERTS

SEA GULL

The sea gull curves his wings,
    the sea gull turns his eyes.
Get down into the water, fish!
    (if you are wise.)

The sea gull slants his wings,
    the sea gull turns his head.
Get deep into the water, fish!
    (or you'll be dead.)

ELIZABETH COATSWORTH

MRS. PECK-PIGEON

Mrs. Peck-Pigeon
Is picking for bread,
Bob—bob—bob
Goes her little round head.
Tame as a pussycat
In the street,
Step—step—step
Go her little red feet.
With her little red feet
And her little round head,
Mrs. Peck-Pigeon
Goes picking for bread.

ELEANOR FARJEON

TREES

Trees are the kindest things I know,

They do no harm, they simply grow

And spread a shade for sleepy cows,

And gather birds among their boughs.

They give us fruit in leaves above,

And wood to make our houses of,

And leaves to burn on Halloween,

And in the Spring new buds of green.

They are first when day's begun

To touch the beams of morning sun,

They are the last to hold the light

When evening changes into night,

And when a moon floats on the sky

They hum a drowsy lullaby

Of sleepy children long ago . . .

Trees are the kindest things I know.

HARRY BEHN

SONG

Elms are proud
and cedars dark,
poplars have silver
leaf-shadowed bark,
aspens whisper,
willows weep,
and all the tree toads
have gone to sleep.

ELIZABETH COATSWORTH

THE
BEECH
TREE

I'd like to have a garden
With a beech tree on the lawn;
The little birds that lived there
Would wake me up at dawn.

And in the summer weather
When all the leaves were green,
I'd sit beneath the beech boughs
And see the sky between.

ROSE FYLEMAN

QUEEN ANNE'S LACE

Queen Anne, Queen Anne, has washed her lace
  (She chose a summer's day)
  And hung it in a grassy place
    To whiten, if it may.

Queen Anne, Queen Anne, has left it there,
    And slept the dewy night;
Then waked, to find the sunshine fair,
    And all the meadows white.

Queen Anne, Queen Anne, is dead and gone
    (She died a summer's day),
    But left her lace to whiten on
    Each weed-entangled way!

MARY LESLIE NEWTON

124

NAMES

Larkspur and Hollyhock,
Pink Rose and purple Stock,
Lovely smelling Mignonette,
Lilies not quite opened yet,
Phlox the favorite of bees,
Bleeding Heart and Peonies—
Just their names are nice to say,
Softly,
On a summer's day.

DOROTHY ALDIS

DANDELIONS

Over the climbing meadows
Where the swallow shadows float,
These are the small gold buttons
On earth's green, windy coat.

FRANCES FROST

125

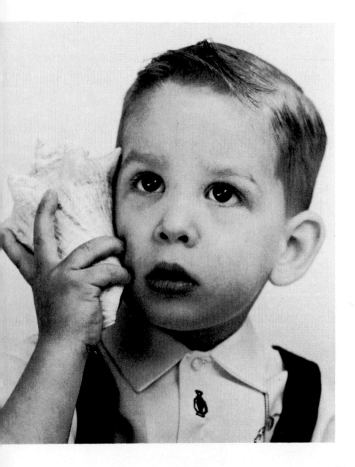

ALONE BY THE SURF

There is no world sound—
Only stillness of stars,
Silence of sand,
A single shell,
By the sliding sea.

LEILA KENDALL BROWN

PALACE

A sea shell is a palace
Where many echoes dwell,
And when I listen to them
I know them all quite well.
They are like the ocean's roar
Where the sea shell buried deep
Learns why the sea is always salt,
And spooky shadows creep.

DOROTHY VENA JOHNSON

R

hymes
of life
at home

SONG FOR A LITTLE HOUSE

I'm glad our house is a little house,
    Not too tall nor too wide:
I'm glad the hovering butterflies
    Feel free to come inside.

Our little house is a friendly house.
    It is not shy or vain;
It gossips with the talking trees,
    And makes friends with the rain.

And quick leaves cast a shimmer of green
    Against our whited walls,
And in the phlox the courteous bees
    Are paying duty calls.

CHRISTOPHER MORLEY

THE SHINY LITTLE HOUSE

I wish, how I wish, that I had a little house,
With a mat for the cat and a hole for the mouse,
And a clock going "tock" in a corner of the room
And a kettle, and a cupboard, and a big birch broom.

To school in the morning the children off would run,
And I'd give them a kiss and a penny and a bun.
But directly they had gone from this little house of mine,
I'd clap my hands and snatch a cloth,
and shine, shine, shine.

I'd shine all the knives, all the windows and the floors,
All the grates, all the plates, all the handles on the doors,
Every fork, every spoon, every lid, and every tin,
Till everything was shining like a new bright pin.

At night, by the fire, when the children were in bed,
I'd sit and I'd knit, with a cap upon my head,
And the kettles and the saucepans,
they would shine, shine, shine,
In this tweeny little, cosy little house of mine!

NANCY M. HAYES

129

MOVING

I like to move. There's such a feeling
Of hurrying
      and scurrying,
And such a feeling
Of men with trunks and packing cases,
Of kitchen clocks and mother's laces,
Dusters, dishes, books, and vases,
Toys and pans and candles.

I always find things I'd forgotten,
An old brown Teddy stuffed with cotton,
Some croquet mallets without handles,
A marble and my worn-out sandals,
A half an engine and a hat . . .
And I like that.

I like to watch the big vans backing,
And the lumbering
      and the cumbering,
And the hammering and the tacking.
I even like the packing!

And that will prove
I like to move!

EUNICE TIETJENS

THE NEW NEIGHBOR

Have you had your tonsils out?
  Do you go to school?
Do you know that there are frogs
  Down by the Willow Pool?

Are you good at cricket?
  Have you got a bat?
Do you know the proper way
  To feed a white rat?

Are there any apples
  On your apple tree?
Do you think your mother
  Will ask me in to tea?

ROSE FYLEMAN

A NEW FRIEND

They've taken in the furniture;
I watched them carefully.
I wondered, "Will there be a child
Just right to play with me?"

So I peeked through the garden fence
(I couldn't wait to see).
I found the little boy next door
Was peeking back at me.

MARJORIE ALLEN ANDERSON

131

SATURDAY SHOPPING

To market, to market,
On Saturday morn,
For prunes and potatoes
And ears of sweet corn,
For bacon and sausage,
For apple and pear.
To market, to market—
Our cupboard is bare!

KATHERINE EDELMAN

MIX A PANCAKE

Mix a pancake,
Stir a pancake,
      Pop it in the pan;

Fry the pancake,
Toss the pancake—
     Catch it if you can.

CHRISTINA ROSSETTI

SHELLING PEAS

I like to shell peas
that are fresh from a shop.
I start at the tail end
instead of the top
so they will explode
with a wonderful pop!

AILEEN FISHER

WHEN YOUNG MELISSA SWEEPS

When young Melissa sweeps a room
I vow she dances with the broom!

She curtsies in a corner brightly
And leads her partner forth politely.

Then up and down in jigs and reels,
With gold dust flying at their heels,

They caper. With a whirl or two
They make the wainscot shine like new;

They waltz beside the hearth, and quick
It brightens, shabby brick by brick.

A gay gavotte across the floor,
A Highland fling from door to door,

And every crack and corner's clean
Enough to suit a dainty queen.

If ever you are full of gloom,
Just watch Melissa sweep a room!

NANCY BYRD TURNER

Meg Wohlberg

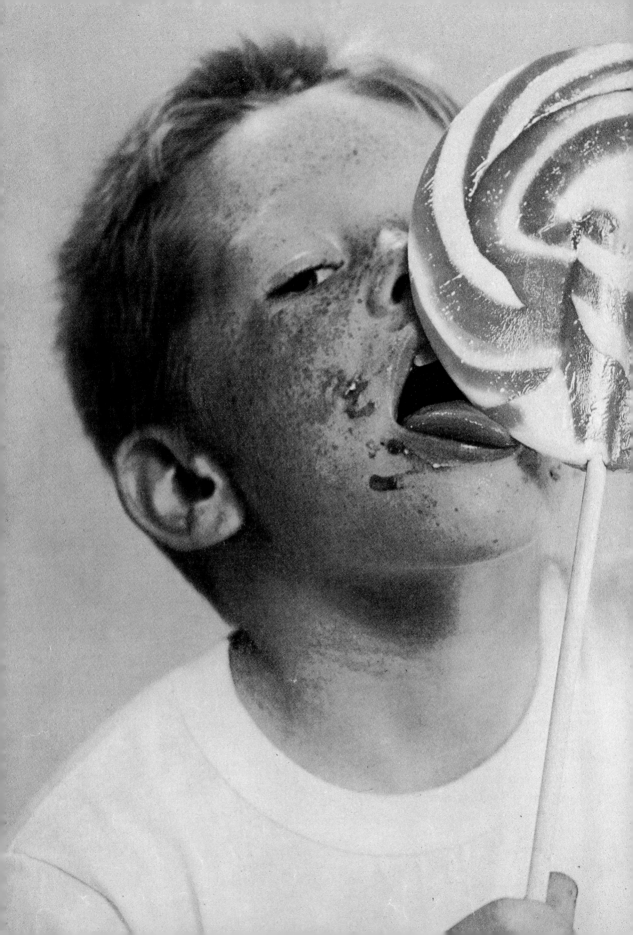

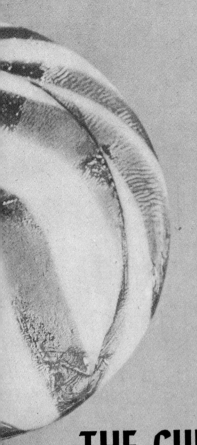

FOOD

When I go walking down the street
There's lots of things I like to eat,

Like pretzels from the pretzel man
And buttered popcorn in a can,

And chocolate peppermints to lick
And candy apples on a stick.

Oh, there are many things to chew
While walking down the avenue.

MARCHETTE CHUTE

THE CUPBOARD

I know a little cupboard,
With a teeny tiny key,
And there's a jar of Lollipops
For me, me, me.

It has a little shelf, my dear,
As dark as dark can be,
And there's a dish of Banbury Cakes
For me, me, me.

I have a small fat grandmamma,
With a very slippery knee,
And she's Keeper of the Cupboard,
With the key, key, key.

And when I'm very good, my dear,
As good as good can be,
There's Banbury Cakes, and Lollipops
For me, me, me.

WALTER DE LA MARE

135

Animal Crackers

Animal crackers, and cocoa to drink,
That is the finest of suppers, I think;
When I'm grown up and can have what I please
I think I shall always insist upon these.

What do *you* choose when *you're* offered a treat?
When Mother says, "What would you like best to eat?"
Is it waffles and syrup, or cinnamon toast?
It's cocoa and animals that *I* love the most!

The kitchen's the coziest place that I know:
The kettle is singing, the stove is aglow,
And there in the twilight, how jolly to see
The cocoa and animals waiting for me.

Daddy and Mother dine later in state,
With Mary to cook for them, Susan to wait;
But they don't have nearly as much fun as I
Who eat in the kitchen with Nurse standing by;
And Daddy once said he would like to be me
Having cocoa and animals once more for tea!

CHRISTOPHER MORLEY

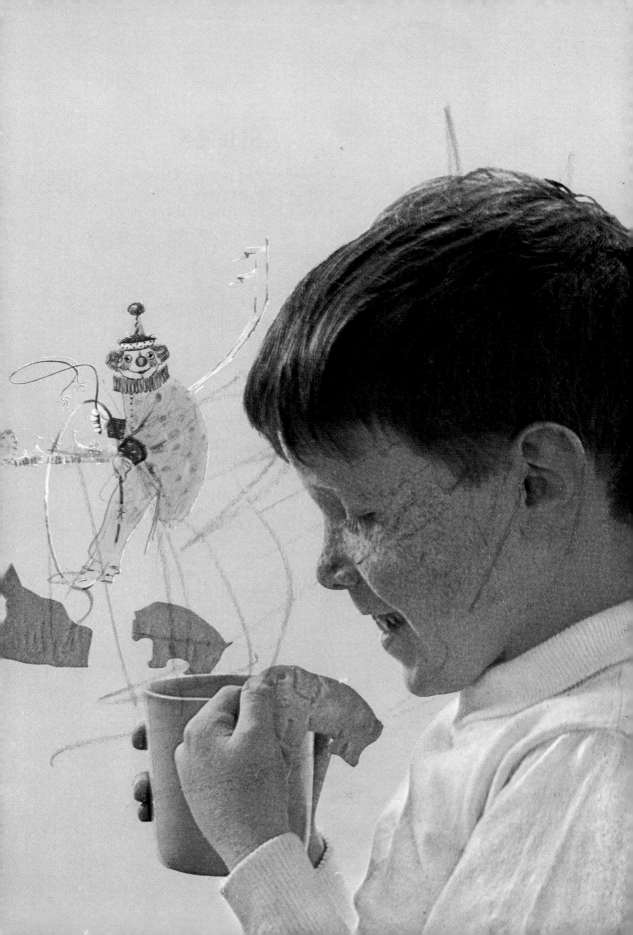

SHOES

My father has a pair of shoes
So beautiful to see!
I want to wear my father's shoes,
They are too big for me.

My baby brother has a pair,
As cunning as can be!
My feet won't go into that pair,
They are too small for me.

There's only one thing I can do
Till I get small or grown.
If I want to have a fitting shoe,
I'll have to wear my own.

TOM ROBINSON

GALOSHES

Susie's galoshes
Make splishes and sploshes
And slooshes and sloshes,
As Susie steps slowly
Along in the slush.

They stamp and they tramp
On the ice and concrete,
They get stuck in the muck and the mud;
But Susie likes much best to hear

The slippery slush
As it slooshes and sloshes,
And splishes and sploshes,
All round her galoshes!

RHODA W. BACMEISTER

138

CHOOSING SHOES

New shoes, new shoes,
    Red and pink and blue shoes.
Tell me, what would *you* choose,
    If they'd let us buy?

Buckle shoes, bow shoes,
    Pretty pointy-toe shoes,
Strappy, cappy low shoes;
    Let's have some to try.

Bright shoes, white shoes,
    Dandy-dance-by-night shoes,
Perhaps-a-little-tight shoes,
    Like some? So would I.

    But

Flat shoes, fat shoes,
    Stump-along-like-that shoes,
Wipe-them-on-the-mat shoes,
    That's the sort they'll buy.

FFRIDA WOLFE

THE MITTEN SONG

(To be chanted)

"Thumbs in the thumb-place,
Fingers all together!"
This is the song
We sing in mitten-weather.
When it is cold,
It doesn't matter whether
Mittens are wool,
Or made of finest leather.
This is the song
We sing in mitten-weather:
"Thumbs in the thumb-place,
Fingers all together!"

MARY LOUISE ALLEN

MY ZIPPER SUIT

My zipper suit is bunny-brown—
The top zips up, the legs zip down.
I wear it every day.
My daddy brought it out from town.
Zip it up, and zip it down,
And hurry out to play!

MARY LOUISE ALLEN

IN WINTER

When I have drunk my orange juice
And cocoa in a cup,
I put my woolly snowsuit on
And get it fastened up.

I go to school and take it off
And hang it on a rack.
And then when recess comes around
I have to hurry back.

And put it on to go and play,
And then when play is through
I take my snowsuit off again—
No easy thing to do.

And when it's time to leave for home
I heave a sigh, and then
I take that woolly suit of mine
And put it on again.

MARCHETTE CHUTE

ABOUT BUTTONS

Every button has a door
Which opens wide to let him in,
But when he rolls upon the floor,
Because he's tired of where he's been
And we can't find him any more,
We use a pin.

DOROTHY ALDIS

SINGING TIME

I wake in the morning early
And always, the very first thing,
I poke out my head and I sit up in bed
And I sing and I sing and I sing.

ROSE FYLEMAN

GROWING

I'm now tall enough
  To reach across the bed;
I put my toes on one side,
  On the other is my head.

L. J. STILES

TIME TO RISE

A birdie with a yellow bill
  Hopped upon the window sill,
Cocked his shining eye and said:
  "Ain't you 'shamed, you sleepyhead?"

ROBERT LOUIS STEVENSON

BREAKFAST TIME

The sun is always in the sky
Whenever I get out of bed,
And I often wonder why
It's never late.—My sister said

She didn't know who did the trick,
And that she didn't care a bit,
And I should eat my porridge quick,
. . . I think its mother wakens it.

JAMES STEPHENS

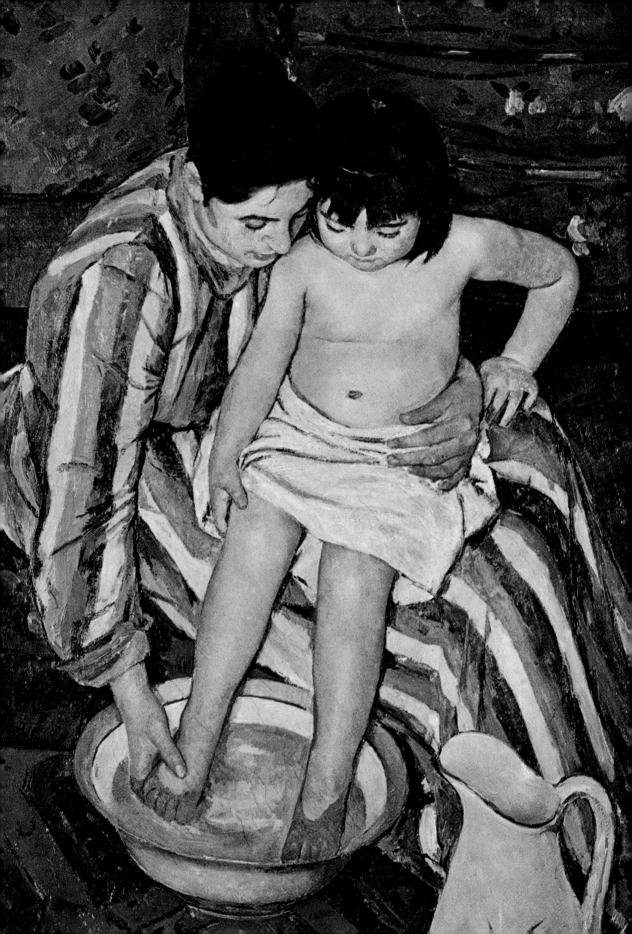

AN INDIGNANT MALE

The way they scrub
Me in the tub,
I think there's
     Hardly
     Any
     Doubt
Sometime they'll rub,
And rub and rub
Until they simply
     Rub
     Me
     Out.

       ABRAM BUNN ROSS

AFTER A BATH

After my bath
I try, try, try
to wipe myself
till I'm dry, dry, dry.

Hands to wipe
and fingers and toes
and two wet legs
and a shiny nose.

Just think how much
less time I'd take
if I were a dog
and could shake, shake, shake.

       AILEEN FISHER

NAUGHTY SOAP SONG

Just when I'm ready to
Start on my ears,
That is the time that my
Soap disappears.

It jumps from my fingers and
Slithers and slides
Down to the end of the
Tub, where it hides.

And acts in a most diso-
Bedient way
AND THAT'S WHY MY SOAP'S GROWING
THINNER EACH DAY.

       DOROTHY ALDIS

JOYS

I'm rather fond of medicine, especially if it's pink,
Or else the fizzy-wizzy kind that makes you want to blink;
And eucalyptus lozenges are very nice I think.

I like it when I'm really ill and have to stay in bed
With mother's grown-up pillows all frilly round my head;
But measles is the funniest, because you get so red.

ROSE FYLEMAN

MUMPS

I had a feeling in my neck,
And on the sides were two big bumps;
I couldn't swallow anything
At all because I had the mumps.

And Mother tied it with a piece,
And then she tied up Will and John,
And no one else but Dick was left
That didn't have a mump rag on.

He teased at us and laughed at us,
And said, whenever he went by,
"It's vinegar and lemon drops
And pickles!" just to make us cry.

But Tuesday Dick was very sad
And cried because his neck was sore,
And not a one said sour things
To anybody any more.

ELIZABETH MADOX ROBERTS

MY BED

I have a little bed
Just for me.
Brother's too big for it.
Mummy's too big for it.
Daddy's *too* big for it.
Do you see?

I have a little bed,
Do you see?
But—pussy's too small for it.
Puppy's too small for it.
Baby's too small for it.
It's *just* for me.

ELIZABETH MANSON SCOTT

HIPPITY HOP TO BED

Oh, it's hippity hop to bed!
I'd rather sit up instead.
But when Father says "must,"
There's nothing but just
Go hippity hop to bed.

LEROY F. JACKSON

IT WAS

When he came to tuck me in
And pat me on the head
He tried to guess (he always does)
Who was in my bed.

"Is it Sally?" he guessed first,
"Or her sister Joan?"
It's such a wriggling little girl
It couldn't be my own.

"It can't be Mary Ann," he said,
"Or Deborah because
All their eyes are much too blue—
My goodness me, I think it's you!"
And he was right. It was.

DOROTHY ALDIS

148

Poems
of play
and
make - believe

smells

Through all the frozen winter
My nose has grown most lonely
For lovely, lovely, colored smells
That come in springtime only

The purple smell of lilacs,
The yellow smell that blows
Across the air of meadows
Where bright forsythia grows.

The tall pink smell of peach trees,
The low white smell of clover,
And everywhere the great green smell
Of grass the whole world over.

KATHRYN WORTH

my nose

It doesn't breathe;
It doesn't smell;
It doesn't feel
So very well.

I am discouraged
With my nose:
The only thing it
Does is blows.

DOROTHY ALDIS

sniff

When school is out, we love to follow
our noses over hill and hollow,
smelling jewelweed and vetch,
sniffing fern and milkweed patch.

The airy fifth of our five senses
leads us under, over, fences.
We run like rabbits through bright hours
and poke our noses into flowers!

FRANCES FROST

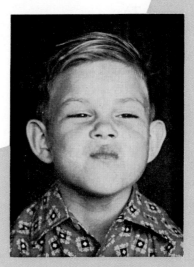

LITTLE

I am the sister of him
And he is my brother.
He is too little for us
To talk to each other.

So every morning I show him
My doll and my book;
But every morning he still is
Too little to look.

DOROTHY ALDIS

THE END

When I was One,
I had just begun.

When I was Two,
I was nearly new.

When I was Three,
I was hardly Me.

When I was Four,
I was not much more.

When I was Five,
I was just alive.

But now I am Six, I'm clever as clever.
So I think I'll be six now for ever and ever.

A. A. MILNE

WHISTLING

Cinda came
up close to hear

How my whistle
sounded NEAR.

And she said,
"I never knew

"You had birds
inside of you."

And poor Cinda
almost cried,

Wishing SHE
had birds inside.

AILEEN FISHER

THREE GUESTS

I had a little tea party,
This afternoon at three;
'Twas very small,
Three guests in all,
Just I, myself, and me.

Myself ate up the sandwiches,
While I drank up the tea,
'Twas also I
Who ate the pie
And passed the cake to me.

JESSICA NELSON NORTH

HIDING

I'm hiding, I'm hiding,
And no one knows where;
For all they can see is my
    Toes and my hair.

And I just heard my father
Say to my mother—
"But, darling, he must be
    Somewhere or other.

"Have you looked in the inkwell?"
And Mother said, "Where?"
"In the INKWELL," said Father. But
    I was not there.

Then "Wait!" cried my mother—
"I think that I see
Him under the carpet." But
    It was not me.

"Inside the mirror's
A pretty good place,"
Said Father and looked, but saw
    Only his face.

"We've hunted," sighed Mother,
"As hard as we could
And I AM so afraid that we've
    Lost him for good."

Then I laughed out aloud
And I wiggled my toes
And Father said—"Look, dear,
    I wonder if those

"Toes could be Benny's.
There are ten of them. See?"
And they WERE so surprised to find
    Out it was me!

DOROTHY ALDIS

"SH"

"Sh!" says Mother,
"Sh!" says Father.
"Running in the hall
Is a very great bother."

"Mrs. Grumpy Grundy,
Who lives down below,
Will come right up
First thing you know."

"Sh!" says Father,
"Sh!" says Mother.
"Can't you play a quiet game
Of some kind or other?"

JAMES S. TIPPETT

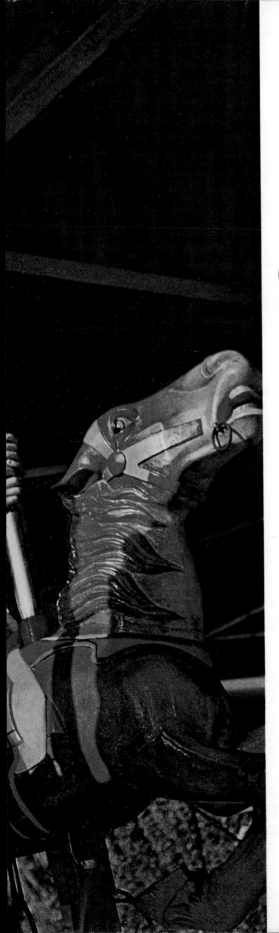

Merry-go-round

I climbed up on the merry-go-round,
And it went round and round.

I climbed up on a big brown horse,
And it went up and down.

Around and round
And up and down,
Around and round
And up and down.

I sat high up
On a big brown horse
And rode around
On the merry-go-round
And rode around

On the merry-go-round
I rode around
On the merry-go-round
Around and round
And round.

DOROTHY W. BARUCH

BEING GYPSY

A gypsy, a gypsy,
Is what I'd like to be,
If ever I could find one who
Would change his place with me.

Rings on my fingers,
Earrings in my ears,
Rough shoes to roam the world
For years and years and years!

I'll be a BAKER

I'll be a baker and run a bakery shop.
I'll bake cookies and never-ever stop.
    "No, ma'am . . . out of bread.
    Have a layer cake instead!
    Have a chocolate cooky spread
    with coconut on top."

"I'll bake pastry all the day long
and put in raisins that maybe don't belong.
    "No, ma'am . . . not a bun.
    Try a crusty pie for fun!
    I've sampled EVERY ONE . . .
    you can't go wrong."

I'll be a baker as soon as I am grown.
"A baker?" mumbles Father, in a curious tone.
    "You ought to be a doctor
    or a lawyer or a chief
    or a banker or a broker,
    but a BAKER—good grief!
    You ought to want an office
    with a desk and telephone . . ."

But I'LL be a baker
    for reasons of my own.

AILEEN FISHER

I'd listen to the stars,
I'd listen to the dawn,
I'd learn the tunes of wind and rain,
The talk of fox and fawn.

A gypsy, a gypsy!
To ramble and to roam
For maybe—oh,
A week or so—
And then I'd hie me home!

BARBARA YOUNG

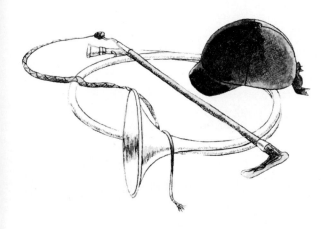

THE HUNTSMEN

Three jolly gentlemen,
　　In coats of red,
Rode their horses
　　Up to bed.

Three jolly gentlemen
　　Snored till morn,
Their horses champing
　　The golden corn.

Three jolly gentlemen,
　　At break of day,
Came clitter-clatter down the stairs
　　And galloped away.

WALTER DE LA MARE

RADIATOR LIONS

George lives in an apartment and
His mother will not let
Him keep a dog or polliwog
Or rabbit for a pet.

So he has Radiator Lions.
(The parlor is their zoo.)
They love to fight but never bite
Unless George tells them to.

But days when it is very cold
And George can't go outdoors
His parlor pets will glower
And crouch upon all fours

And roar most awful roarings.
The noise is very bad.
Up their noses water goeses—
That's what makes them mad.

But he loves Radiator Lions.
He's glad, although they're wild,
He hasn't dogs or polliwogs
Like any other child.

DOROTHY ALDIS

I CAN BE A TIGER

I can't go walking
When they say no,
And I can't go riding
Unless they go.
I can't splash puddles
In my shiny new shoes,
But I can be a tiger
Whenever I choose.

I can't eat peanuts
And I can't eat cake,
I have to go to bed
When they stay awake.
I can't bang windows
And I mustn't tease,
But I can be an elephant
As often as I please.

MILDRED LEIGH ANDERSON

161

A SWING SONG

Swing, swing,
Sing, sing,
Here's my throne, and I am a king!
Swing, sing,
Swing, sing,
Farewell, earth, for I'm on the wing!
Low, high,
Here I fly,
Like a bird through a sunny sky;
Free, free,
Over the lea,
Over the mountain, over the sea!
Up, down,
Up and down,
Which is the way to London Town?
Where, where?
Up in the air,
Close your eyes, and now you are there!
Soon, soon,
Afternoon,
Over the sunset, over the moon;
Far, far,
Over all bar,
Sweeping on from star to star!
No, no,
Low, low,
Sweeping daisies with my toe.
Slow, slow,
To and fro,
Slow—
Slow——
Slow———
Slow.

WILLIAM ALLINGHAM

QUOITS

In wintertime I have such fun
When I play quoits with Father.
I beat him almost every game.
He never seems to bother.

He looks at Mother and just smiles.
All this seems strange to me,
For when he plays with grown-up folks,
He beats them easily.

MARY EFFIE LEE NEWSOME

JUMPING ROPE

The High Skip,
The Sly Skip,
The Skip like a Feather,
The Long Skip,
The Strong Skip,
And the Skip All Together!

The Slow Skip,
The Toe Skip,
The Skip Double-Double,
The Fast Skip,
The Last Skip,
And the Skip Against Trouble!

ELEANOR FARJEON

SLIDING

Down the slide
We ride, we ride.
Round we run, and then
Up we pop
To reach the top,
Down we come again.

MARCHETTE CHUTE

HOPPITY

Cristopher Robin goes
Hoppity, hoppity,

Hoppity, hoppity, hop.
Whenever I tell him
Politely to stop it, he
Says he can't possibly stop.

If he stopped hopping,
he couldn't go anywhere,
Poor little Christopher
Couldn't go anywhere . . .
That's why he *always* goes

Hoppity, hoppity,
Hoppity,
Hoppity,
Hop.

A. A. MILNE

KITE DAYS

A kite, a sky, and a good firm breeze,
And acres of ground away from trees,
And one hundred yards of clean, strong string—
O boy, O boy! I call that Spring!

MARK SAWYER

THE PICNIC

We brought a rug for sitting on,
Our lunch was in a box.
The sand was warm. We didn't wear
Hats or shoes or socks.

Waves came curling up the beach.
We waded. It was fun.
Our sandwiches were different kinds.
I dropped my jelly one.

DOROTHY ALDIS

THE PASTURE

I'm going out to clean the pasture spring;
I'll only stop to rake the leaves away
(And wait to watch the water clear, I may):
I sha'n't be gone long.—You come too.

I'm going out to fetch the little calf
That's standing by the mother. It's so young,
It totters when she licks it with her tongue.
I sha'n't be gone long.—You come too.

ROBERT FROST

SHORE

Play on the seashore
And gather up shells,
Kneel in the damp sands
Digging wells.

Run on the rocks
Where the seaweed slips,
Watch the waves
And the beautiful ships.

MARY BRITTON MILLER

drinking
fountain

When I climb up
To get a drink,
It doesn't work
The way you'd think.

I turn it up.
The water goes
And hits me right
Upon the nose.

I turn it down
To make it small
And don't get any
Drink at all.

MARCHETTE CHUTE

sprinkling

Sometimes in the summer
When the day is hot
Daddy takes the garden hose
And finds a shady spot;
Then he calls me over,
Looks at my bare toes
And says, "Why, you need sprinkling,
You thirsty little rose!"

DOROTHY MASON PIERCE

mud

Mud is very nice to feel
All squishy-squash between the toes!
I'd rather wade in wiggly mud
Than smell a yellow rose.

Nobody else but the rosebush knows
How nice mud feels
Between the toes.

POLLY CHASE BOYDEN

skating

When I try to skate,
My feet are so wary
They grit and they grate:
And then I watch Mary
Easily gliding,
Like an ice fairy;
Skimming and curving,
Out and in,
With a turn of her head,
And a lift of her chin,
And a gleam of her eye,
And a twirl and a spin;
Sailing under
The breathless hush
Of the willows, and back
To the frozen rush;
Out to the island
And round the edge,

Skirting the rim
Of the crackling sedge,
Swerving close
To the poplar root,
And round the lake
On a single foot,
With a three, and an eight,
And a loop and a ring;
Where Mary glides,
The lake will sing!
Out in the mist
I hear her now
Under the frost
Of the willow bough
Easily sailing,
Light and fleet,
With the song of the lake
Beneath her feet.

HERBERT ASQUITH

169

the land of counterpane

When I was sick and lay a-bed,
I had two pillows at my head,
And all my toys beside me lay
To keep me happy all the day.

And sometimes for an hour or so
I watched my leaden soldiers go,
With different uniforms and drills,
Among the bedclothes, through the hills;

And sometimes sent my ships in fleets
All up and down among the sheets;
Or brought my trees and houses out,
And planted cities all about.

I was the giant great and still
That sits upon the pillow-hill,
And sees before him, dale and plain,
The pleasant land of counterpane.

ROBERT LOUIS STEVENSON

wings
and wheels

Ahoy and ahoy, birds!
We cannot have wings
And feathers and things,
But dashing on wheels
With the wind at our heels
Is almost like flying—
Such joy, birds!

Oho and Oho, birds!
Of course we can't rise
Up and up to the skies;
But skimming and sliding
On rollers, and gliding,
Is almost as jolly,
You know, birds!

NANCY BYRD TURNER

170

leisure

What is this life if, full of care,
We have no time to stand and stare.

No time to stand beneath the boughs
And stare as long as sheep or cows.

No time to see, when woods we pass,
Where squirrels hide their nuts in grass.

No time to see, in broad daylight,
Streams full of stars, like stars at night.

No time to turn at Beauty's glance,
And watch her feet, how they can dance.

No time to wait till her mouth can
Enrich that smile her eyes began.

A poor life this if, full of care,
We have no time to stand and stare.

WILLIAM HENRY DAVIES

HALFWAY DOWN

Halfway down the stairs
　Is a stair
　　Where I sit.
　　　There isn't any
　　　　Other stair
　　　　　Quite like
　　　　　　It.
　　　　　　　I'm not at the bottom,
　　　　　　　I'm not at the top;
　　　　　　　　So this is the stair
　　　　　　　　Where
　　　　　　　　　I always
　　　　　　　　　　Stop.

　　　　　　　Halfway up the stairs
　　　　　　　　Isn't up,
　　　　　　　　　And isn't down.
　　　　　　　　　It isn't in the nursery,
　　　　　　　　　It isn't in the town.
　　　　　　　　　And all sorts of funny thoughts
　　　　　　　　　Run around my head:
　　　　　　　　　"It isn't really
　　　　　　　　　　Anywhere!
　　　　　　　　　　　It's somewhere else
　　　　　　　　　　　Instead!"

A. A. MILNE

poems
about
pets
and

G rownups

THE ANIMAL STORE

If I had a hundred dollars to spend,
    Or maybe a little more,
I'd hurry as fast as my legs would go
    Straight to the animal store.

I wouldn't say, "How much for this or that?"
    "What kind of dog is he?"
I'd buy as many as rolled an eye,
    Or wagged a tail at me!

I'd take the hound with the drooping ears
    That sits by himself alone;
Cockers and Cairns and wobbly pups
    For to be my very own.

I might buy a parrot all red and green,
    And the monkey I saw before,
If I had a hundred dollars to spend,
    Or maybe a little more.

RACHEL FIELD

175

His nose is short and scrubby;
His ears hang rather low;
And he always brings the stick back,
No matter how far you throw.

MY DOG

He gets spanked rather often
For things he shouldn't do,
Like lying-on-beds, and barking,
And eating up shoes when they're new.

He always wants to be going
Where he isn't supposed to go.
He tracks up the house when it's snowing—
Oh, puppy, I love you so.

MARCHETTE CHUTE

He sits and begs, he gives a paw,
He is, as you can see,
The finest dog you ever saw,
And he belongs to me.

He follows everywhere I go
And even when I swim.
I laugh because he thinks, you know,
That I belong to him.

But still no matter what we do
We never have a fuss;
And so I guess it must be true
That *we* belong to *us*.

ARTHUR GUITERMAN

CHUMS

Puppy And I

I met a Man as I went walking;
We got talking,
Man and I.
"Where are you going to, Man?" I said
   (I said to the Man as he went by).
"Down to the village, to get some bread.
Will you come with me?" "No, not I."

I met a Horse as I went walking;
We got talking,
Horse and I.
"Where are you going to, Horse, today?"
   (I said to the Horse as he went by).
"Down to the village to get some hay.
Will you come with me?" "No, not I."

I met a Woman as I went walking;
We got talking,
Woman and I.
"Where are you going to, Woman, so early?"
   (I said to the Woman as she went by).
"Down to the village to get some barley.
Will you come with me?" "No, not I."

I met some Rabbits as I went walking;
We got talking,
Rabbits and I.
"Where are you going in your brown fur coats?"
    (I said to the Rabbits as they went by).
"Down to the village to get some oats.
Will you come with us?" "No, not I."

I met a Puppy as I went walking;
We got talking,
Puppy and I.
"Where are you going this nice fine day?"
    (I said to the Puppy as he went by).
"Up in the hills to roll and play."
"*I'll* come with you, Puppy," said I.

A. A. MILNE

179

FORGIVEN

I found a little beetle, so that Beetle was his name,
And I called him Alexander and he answered just the same.
I put him in a match-box, and I kept him all the day . . .
And Nanny let my beetle out—
    Yes, Nanny let my beetle out—
    She went and let my beetle out—
    And Beetle ran away.

She said she didn't mean it, and I never said she did,
She said she wanted matches and she just took off the lid,
She said that she was sorry, but it's difficult to catch
An excited sort of beetle you've mistaken for a match.

She said that she was sorry, and I really mustn't mind,
As there's lots and lots of beetles which she's certain we could find,
If we looked about the garden for the holes where beetles hid—
And we'd get another match-box and write BEETLE on the lid.

We went to all the places which a beetle might be near,
And we made the sort of noises which a beetle likes to hear,
And I saw a kind of something, and I gave a sort of shout:
"A beetle-house and Alexander Beetle coming out!"

It was Alexander Beetle I'm as certain as can be
And he had a sort of look as if he thought it must be ME,
And he had a sort of look as if he thought he ought to say:
"I'm very very sorry that I tried to run away."

And Nanny's very sorry too for you-know-what-she-did,
And she's writing ALEXANDER very blackly on the lid.
So Nan and Me are friends, because it's difficult to catch
An excited Alexander you've mistaken for a match.

A. A. MILNE

CAT

The black cat yawns,
Opens her jaws,
Stretches her legs,
And shows her claws.

Then she gets up
And stands on four
Long stiff legs
And yawns some more.

She shows her sharp teeth,
She stretches her lip,
Her slice of a tongue
Turns up at the tip.

Lifting herself
On her delicate toes,
She arches her back
As high as it goes.

She lets herself down
With particular care,
And pads away
With her tail in the air.

182   MARY BRITTON MILLER

THE MYSTERIOUS CAT

I saw a proud, mysterious cat,
I saw a proud, mysterious cat,
Too proud to catch a mouse or rat—
    Mew, mew, mew.

But catnip she would eat, and purr,
But catnip she would eat, and purr.
And goldfish she did much prefer—
    Mew, mew, mew.

I saw a cat—'twas but a dream,
I saw a cat—'twas but a dream,
    Who scorned the slave
    that brought her cream—
    Mew, mew, mew.

Unless the slave were dressed in style,
Unless the slave were dressed in style,
And knelt before her all the while—
Mew, mew, mew.

Did you ever hear of a thing like that?
Did you ever hear of a thing like that?
Did you ever hear of a thing like that?
Oh, what a proud mysterious cat.
Oh, what a proud mysterious cat.
Oh, what a proud mysterious cat.
Mew . . . mew . . . mew.

VACHEL LINDSAY

everybody says

Everybody says
I look just like my mother.
Everybody says
I'm the image of Aunt Bee.
Everybody says
My nose is like my father's.
But *I* want to look like ME!

DOROTHY ALDIS

walking

When Daddy
Walks
With Jean and me,
We have a
Lot of fun
'Cause we can't
Walk as fast
As he,
Unless we
Skip and
Run!
I stretch,
And stretch
My legs so far,
I nearly slip
And fall—
But how
Does Daddy
Take such steps?
He doesn't stretch
At all!

GRACE GLAUBITZ

daddy

When Daddy shaves and lets me stand and look,
I like it better than a picture book.
He pulls such lovely faces all the time
Like funny people in a pantomime.

ROSE FYLEMAN

dresses

When my mother is not there
Her dresses hang so sadly
In the closet near the stair,
For they are feeling badly.

They look so straight when she is gone,
They're droopier and thinner;
They have a kind of patient look—
As though they needed dinner.

DOROTHY ALDIS

UNCLE FRANK

It's queer about my Uncle Frank,
He sits and figures in a bank,
When he might keep a candy store—
A shining sign above the door.
Or he might keep a big toy shop
With things that fly and skip and hop—
With trailer trucks and things that crank,
Instead of working in a bank.

MONICA SHANNON

GREATY-GREAT GRANNIE

My Greaty-great Grannie is terribly small
And she smells just like a sachet.
She twinkles and she winkles
And she's full of funny wrinkles
But she always has a pretzel tucked away!

My Greaty-great Grannie is terribly old.
I guess she's as old as can be.
She teases and she squeezes
And she sneezes funny sneezes
But she always has a pretzel just for me!

LYSBETH BOYD BORIE

DOORBELLS

You never know with a doorbell
Who may be ringing it—
It may be Great-Aunt Cynthia
To spend the day and knit;
It may be a peddler with things to sell
(I'll buy some when I'm older),
Or the grocer's boy with his apron on
And a basket on his shoulder;
It may be the old umbrella man
Giving his queer, cracked call,
Or a lady dressed in rustly silk,
With cardcase and parasol.
Doorbells are like a magic game,
Or the grab bag at a fair—
You never know when you hear one ring
Who may be waiting there!

RACHEL FIELD

187

AT MRS. APPLEBY'S

When frost is shining on the trees,
  It's spring at Mrs. Appleby's.
You smell it in the air before
  You step inside the kitchen door.

Rows of scarlet flowers bloom
  From every window in the room.
And funny little speckled fish
  Are swimming in a china dish.

A tiny bird with yellow wings
  Just sits and sings and sings and SINGS.
Outside when frost is on the trees,
  It's spring at Mrs. Appleby's!

ELIZABETH UPHAM MCWEBB

MISS T.

It's a very odd thing—
  As odd as can be—
That whatever Miss T. eats
  Turns into Miss T.;
Porridge and apples,
  Mince, muffins, and mutton,
Jam, junket, jumbles—
  Not a rap, not a button
It matters; the moment
  They're out of her plate,
Though shared by Miss Butcher
  And sour Mr. Bate;
Tiny and cheerful,
  And neat as can be,
Whatever Miss T. eats
  Turns into Miss T.

WALTER DE LA MARE

189

LIKE ME

A garbage man is a garbage man
Who rattles and bangs the garbage can.

Like me.

A policeman carries a club in his hand.

Like me.

The mailman carries a bag. Like mine.
And they all of them always have a good time.

Like me.

DOROTHY ALDIS

P'S THE PROUD POLICEMAN

P's the proud Policeman
With buttons polished neat.
He's pleased to put his hand up
When you want to cross the street.
By daylight he protects you;
He protects you through the dark,
And he points the way politely
To the playground or the park.

PHYLLIS McGINLEY

MY POLICEMAN

He is always standing there
At the corner of the Square;
He is very big and fine
And his silver buttons shine.

All the carts and taxis do
Everything he tells them to,
And the little errand boys
When they pass him make no noise.

Though I seem so very small
I am not afraid at all;
He and I are friends, you see,
And he always smiles at me.

ROSE FYLEMAN

191

THE
ICE-CREAM
MAN

When summer's in the city,
    And brick's a blaze of heat,
The Ice-Cream Man with his little cart
    Goes trundling down the street.

Beneath his round umbrella,
    Oh, what a joyful sight,
To see him fill the cones with mounds
    Of cooling brown or white:

Vanilla, chocolate, strawberry,
    Or chilly things to drink
From bottles full of frosty fizz,
    Green, orange, white, or pink.

His cart might be a flowerbed
    Of roses and sweet peas,
The way the children cluster round
    As thick as honeybees.

RACHEL FIELD

THE COBBLER

Crooked heels
  And scuffy toes
Are all the kinds
  Of shoes he knows.

He patches up
  The broken places,
Sews the seams
  And shines their faces.

ELEANOR A. CHAFFEE

THE DENTIST

I'd like to be a dentist with a plate upon the door
And a little bubbling fountain in the middle of the floor;
With lots of tiny bottles all arranged in colored rows
And a page boy with a line of silver buttons down his clothes.

I'd love to polish up the things and put them every day
Inside the darling chests of drawers all tidily away;
And every Sunday afternoon when nobody was there
I should go riding up and down upon the velvet chair.

ROSE FYLEMAN

ONLY ONE MOTHER

Hundreds of stars in the pretty sky,
Hundreds of shells on the shore together,
Hundreds of birds that go singing by,
Hundreds of lambs in the sunny weather.

Hundreds of dewdrops to greet the dawn,
Hundreds of bees in the purple clover,
Hundreds of butterflies on the lawn,
But only one mother the wide world over.

GEORGE COOPER

highway,
byway,
and
City rhymes

Maps

High adventure
   And bright dream—
Maps are mightier
   Than they seem:

Ships that follow
   Leaning stars—
Red and gold of
   Strange bazaars—

Ice floes hid
   Beyond all knowing—
Planes that ride where
   Winds are blowing!

Train maps, maps of
   Wind and weather,
Road maps—taken
   Altogether

Maps are really
   Magic wands
For home-staying
   Vagabonds!

DOROTHY BROWN THOMPSON

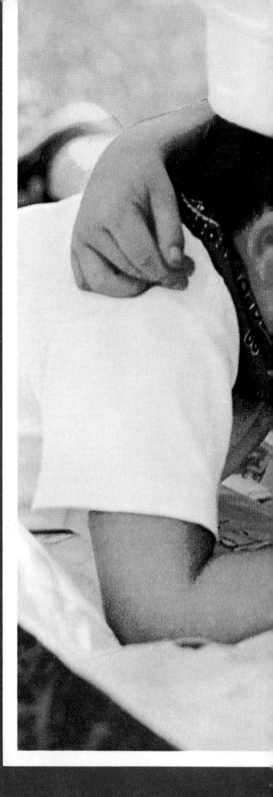

OPEN RANGE

Prairie goes to the mountain,
Mountain goes to the sky.
The sky sweeps across to the distant hills
And here, in the middle,
Am I.

       Hills crowd down to the river,
       River runs by the tree.
       Tree throws its shadow on sunburnt grass
       And here, in the shadow,
       Is me.

              Shadows creep up the mountain,
              Mountain goes black on the sky,
              The sky bursts out with a million stars
              And here, by the campfire,
              Am I.

                                        KATHRYN AND BYRON JACKSON

WESTERN WAGONS

They went with axe and rifle,
    when the trail was still to blaze,
They went with wife and children,
    in the prairie-schooner days,
With banjo and with frying pan—
    Susanna, don't you cry!
For I'm off to California
    to get rich out there or die!

We've broken land and cleared it,
    but we're tired of where we are.
They say that wild Nebraska
    is a better place by far.
There's gold in far Wyoming,
    there's black earth in Ioway,
So pack up the kids and blankets,
    for we're moving out today!

The cowards never started
    and the weak died on the road,
And all across the continent
    the endless campfires glowed.
We'd taken land and settled—
    but a traveler passed by—
And we're going West tomorrow—
    Lordy, never ask us why!

We're going West tomorrow,
    where the promises can't fail.
O'er the hills in legions, boys,
    and crowd the dusty trail!
We shall starve and freeze and suffer.
    We shall die, and tame the lands.
But we're going West tomorrow,
    with our fortune in our hands.

ROSEMARY AND STEPHEN VINCENT BENÉT

STOP - GO

Automobiles
In
a
row
Wait to go
While the signal says:
STOP

Bells ring
Ting-a-ling
Red light's gone!
Green light's on!
Horns blow!
And the row
Starts
to
GO

DOROTHY W. BARUCH

TAXIS

Ho, for taxis green or blue,
Hi, for taxis red,
They roll along the Avenue
Like spools of colored thread!

Jack-o'-Lantern yellow,
Orange as the moon,
Greener than the greenest grass
Ever grew in June.
Gaily striped or checked in squares,
Wheels that twinkle bright,
Don't you think that taxis make
A very pleasant sight?
Taxis shiny in the rain,
Scudding through the snow,
Taxis flashing back the sun
Waiting in a row.

Ho, for taxis red and green,
Hi, for taxis blue,
I wouldn't be a private car
In sober black, would you?

RACHEL FIELD

GOOD GREEN BUS

Rumbling and rattly good green Bus
Where are you going to carry us?
Up the shiny lengths of Avenue
Where lights keep company two by two;
Where windows glitter with things to buy,
And churches hold their steeples high.
Round the Circle and past the Park,
Still and shadowy, dim and dark,
Over the asphalt and into the Drive—
Isn't it fun to be alive?
Look to the left and the River's there
With ships and whistles and freshened air;
To the right—more windows, row on row,
And everyone like a picture show,
Or little stages where people play
At being themselves by night and day,
And never guess that they have us
For audience in the good green Bus!

RACHEL FIELD

MOTOR CARS

From a city window, 'way up high,
I like to watch the cars go by.
They look like burnished beetles, black,
That leave a little muddy track
Behind them as they slowly crawl.
Sometimes they do not move at all
But huddle close with hum and drone
As though they feared to be alone.
They grope their way through fog and night
With the golden feelers of their light.

ROWENA BASTIN BENNETT

203

CITY STREETS
AND
COUNTRY ROADS

The city has streets—
  But the country has roads.
In the country one meets
  Blue carts with their loads
Of sweet-smelling hay,
  And mangolds, and grain:
Oh, take me away
  To the country again!

In the city one sees
  Big trams rattle by,
And the breath of the chimneys
  That blot out the sky,
And all down the pavements
  Stiff lamp-posts one sees—
But the country has hedgerows,
  The country has trees.

As sweet as the sun
  In the country is rain:
Oh, take me away
  To the country again!

ELEANOR FARJEON

204

COUNTRY TRUCKS

Big trucks with apples
And big trucks with grapes
Thundering through the mountains
While every wild thing gapes.

Thundering through the valley,
Like something just let loose,
Big trucks with oranges
For city children's juice.

Big trucks with peaches,
And big trucks with pears,
Frightening all the rabbits
And giving squirrels gray hairs.

Yet, when city children
Sit down to plum or prune,
They know more trucks are coming
As surely as the moon.

MONICA SHANNON

THE
WAYS
OF
TRAINS

I hear the engine pounding
in triumph down the track—
trains take away the ones you love
and then they bring them back!

trains take away the ones you love
to worlds both strange and new
and then, with care and courtesy,
they bring them back to you.

The engine halts and snuffs and snorts,
it breathes forth smoke and fire,
then snatches crowded strangers on—
but leaves what you desire!

ELIZABETH COATSWORTH

TRAINS
AT
NIGHT

I like the whistle of trains at night,
The fast trains thundering by so proud!
They rush and rumble across the world,
They ring wild bells and they toot so loud!

But I love better the slow trains.
They take their time through the world instead,
And whistle softly and stop to tuck
Each sleepy blinking town in bed!

FRANCES FROST

I'D LIKE TO BE
A LIGHTHOUSE

I'd like to be a lighthouse
All scrubbed and painted white.
I'd like to be a lighthouse
And stay awake all night
To keep my eye on everything
That sails my patch of sea;
I'd like to be a lighthouse
With the ships all watching me.

RACHEL FIELD

WHERE GO THE BOATS?

Dark brown is the river
   Golden is the sand.
It flows along forever,
   With trees on either hand.

Green leaves a-floating,
   Castles of the foam,
Boats of mine a-boating—
   Where will all come home?

On goes the river
   And out past the mill,
Away down the valley,
   Away down the hill.

Away down the river,
   A hundred miles or more,
Other little children
   Shall bring my boats ashore.

ROBERT LOUIS STEVENSON

UP IN THE AIR

Zooming across the sky
Like a great bird you fly,
    Airplane,
    Silvery white
    In the light.

Turning and twisting in air,
When shall I ever be there,
    Airplane,
    Piloting you
    Far in the blue?

JAMES S. TIPPETT

BUILDING A SKYSCRAPER

They're building a skyscraper
Near our street.
Its height will be nearly
One thousand feet.

It covers completely
A city block.
They drilled its foundation
Through solid rock.

They made its framework
Of great steel beams
With riveted joints
And welded seams.

A swarm of workmen
Strain and strive
Like busy bees
In a honeyed hive

Building the skyscraper
Into the air
While crowds of people
Stand and stare.

Higher and higher
The tall towers rise
Like Jacob's ladder
Into the skies.

JAMES S. TIPPETT

CITY

In the morning the city
Spreads its wings
Making a song
In stone that sings.

In the evening the city
Goes to bed
Hanging lights
About its head.

LANGSTON HUGHES

SKYSCRAPER IS A CITY'S HOUSE

Skyscraper is a City's house
Only a city would need to build a house to reach the clouds
Only a city would dare to raise a building twelve hundred
feet into the air
Only a city of many roads could summon stone and cement,
chromium and steel
Only a city of myriad workers could fashion the complex giant,
could rear a house of a hundred stories in twenty months,
a house strong to shelter eighty thousand people.
SKYSCRAPER is a city's house!

ELSA NAUMBURG, CLARA LAMBERT, AND LUCY SPRAGUE

213

ELEVATOR →

the ELEVATOR

The elevator
In the store
Has a door
That slides
Open—closed.

Then the driver moves a handle,
And up and up
The elevator slips
And *stops*
And *out* go some people
And *in* come some people.

And up and up the elevator slips
And stops
And out go some people
And in come some people.
And down and *down*
The elevator drops
To the floor
Where I
Get out.

DOROTHY W. BARUCH

EXIT →

214

HOLD HAND RAIL

E is the
ESCALATOR

E is the Escalator
 That gives an elegant ride.
You step on the stair
With an easy air
 And up and up you glide.
It's nicer than scaling ladders
 Or scrambling 'round a hill,
For you climb and climb
But all the time
You're really standing still.

PHYLLIS McGINLEY

215

THE TELEGRAPH

The wires spread out far and wide,
And cross the town and countryside,
They cross through deserts and through snows,
And pass the spots where no one goes.

But though no feet go out that way
A million words go every day;
Along the wires everywhere
A million words flash through the air.

And if we're happy, if we're well,
The wires far away can tell,
The little words can cross all space
And talk to friends in any place.

ANNETTE WYNNE

A LETTER IS A GYPSY ELF

A letter is a gypsy elf
It goes where I would go myself;
East or West or North, it goes,
Or South past pretty bungalows,
Over mountain, over hill,
Any place it must and will,
It finds good friends that live so far
You cannot travel where they are.

ANNETTE WYNNE

MAIL

Writing a letter
Is really quite fun
Because I can mail it
As soon as it's done.

MARCHETTE CHUTE

THE WORLD

Great, wide, beautiful,
   wonderful World,
With the wonderful water
   round you curled,
And the wonderful grass
   upon your breast,
World, you are beautifully drest.

WILLIAM BRIGHTY RANDS

OTHERWISE

There must be magic,
Otherwise,
How could day turn to night,

And how could sailboats,
Otherwise,
Go sailing out of sight,

And how could peanuts,
Otherwise,
Be covered up so tight?

AILEEN FISHER

Verses just for fun

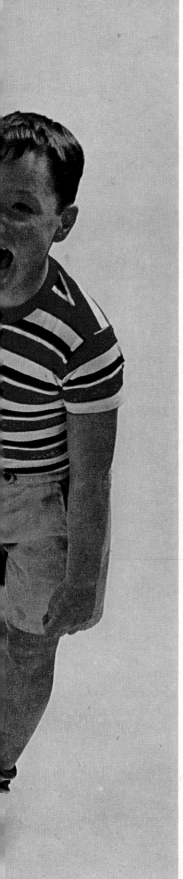

LAUGHING SONG

Come live and be merry,
and join with me,
To sing the sweet chorus
of "Ha, ha, he!"

WILLIAM BLAKE

THE LITTLE LAND

When at home alone I sit,
And am very tired of it,
I have just to shut my eyes
To go sailing through the skies—
To go sailing far away
To the pleasant Land of Play.

ROBERT LOUIS STEVENSON

CIRCLES

The things to draw with compasses
Are suns and moons and circleses
And rows of humptydumpasses
Or anything in circuses
Like hippopotamusseses
And hoops and camels' humpasses
And wheels on clownses busseses
And fat old elephumpasses.

HARRY BEHN

THE VULTURE

The Vulture eats between his meals,
And that's the reason why
He very, very rarely feels
As well as you and I.
His eye is dull, his head is bald,
His neck is growing thinner.
Oh! what a lesson for us all
To only eat at dinner!

HILAIRE BELLOC

THE PURPLE COW

I never Saw a Purple Cow,
I never Hope to See One;
But I can Tell you, Anyhow,
I'd rather See than Be One.

GELETT BURGESS

HORSIES MAKE HORSIES

Horsies make horsies
And ants make ants.
And elephants
Make elephants.
But bees make honey,
Isn't it funny?

JOHN LEONARD BECKER

223

LIMERICKS

There Was an Old Person of Ware

There was an old person of Ware,
Who rode on the back of a bear;
When they said, "Does it trot?"
He said: "Certainly not,
It's a Moppsikon Floppsikon bear."

EDWARD LEAR

There Was an Old Man with a Beard

There was an old man with a beard,
Who said, "It is just as I feared!
Two Owls and a Hen
Four Larks and a Wren
Have all built their nests in my beard."

EDWARD LEAR

There Was a Young Maid Who Said, "Why"

There was a young maid who said, "Why
Can't I look in my ear with my eye?
If I give my mind to it,
I'm sure I can do it,
You never can tell till you try."

EDWARD LEAR

ELETELEPHONY

Once there was an elephant,
Who tried to use the telephant—
No! no! I mean an elephone
Who tried to use the telephone—
(Dear me! I am not certain quite
That even now I've got it right.)

Howe'er it was, he got his trunk
Entangled in the telephunk;
The more he tried to get it free,
The louder buzzed the telephee—
(I fear I'd better drop the song
Of elephop and telephong!)

LAURA E. RICHARDS

THE OWL AND THE PUSSYCAT

The Owl and the Pussycat went to sea
In a beautiful pea-green boat,
They took some honey, and plenty of money,
Wrapped up in a five-pound note.
The Owl looked up to the stars above,
And sang to a small guitar,
"O lovely Pussy! O Pussy, my love,
What a beautiful Pussy you are,
You are,
You are!
What a beautiful Pussy you are!"

Pussy said to the Owl, "You elegant fowl!
How charmingly sweet you sing!
O let us be married! too long we have tarried:
But what shall we do for a ring?"
They sailed away for a year and a day,
To the land where the Bong-tree grows;
And there in a wood a Piggy-wig stood,
With a ring at the end of his nose,
His nose,
His nose,
With a ring at the end of his nose.

"Dear Pig, are you willing to sell for one shilling
Your ring?" Said the Piggy, "I will."
So they took it away, and were married next day
By the Turkey who lives on the hill.
They dined on mince, and slices of quince,
Which they ate with a runcible spoon;
And hand in hand, on the edge of the sand,
They danced by the light of the moon,
The moon,
The moon,
They danced by the light of the moon.

EDWARD LEAR

THE MONKEYS
AND THE
CROCODILE

Five little monkeys
Swinging from a tree;
Teasing Uncle Crocodile,
Merry as can be.
Swinging high, swinging low,
Swinging left and right:
"Dear Uncle Crocodile,
Come and take a bite!"

Five little monkeys
Swinging in the air;
Heads up, tails up
Little do they care.
Swinging up, swinging down,
Swinging far and near:
"Poor Uncle Crocodile,
Aren't you hungry, dear?"

Four little monkeys
Sitting in the tree;
Heads down, tails down,
Dreary as can be.
Weeping loud, weeping low,
Crying to each other:
"Wicked Uncle Crocodile,
To gobble up our brother!"

LAURA E. RICHARDS

TWENTY FROGGIES

Twenty froggies went to school
Down beside a rushy pool.
Twenty little coats of green,
Twenty vests all white and clean.

"We must be in time," said they,
"First we study, then we play.
That is how we keep the rule,
When we froggies go to school."

Master Bullfrog, brave and stern,
Called his classes in their turn,
Taught them how to nobly strive,
Also how to leap and dive;

Taught them how to dodge a blow
From the sticks that bad boys throw.
Twenty froggies grew up fast,
Bullfrogs they became at last;

Polished in a high degree,
As each froggie ought to be,
Now they sit on other logs,
Teaching other little frogs.

GEORGE COOPER

ROAD FELLOWS

Little Tillie Turtle
Went a-walking down the road
And happened at the corner
On little Tommy Toad.
"Good-morning, Sir," said Tillie.
"Good-morning, Ma'am," said he,
And they strolled along together
As cosy as could be.

And when they reached the orchard,
As sure as you're alive,
They saw big Billy Bumble-bee
Emerging from his hive.
"Good-morning, friends," said Billy.
"Good-morning, Sir," said they.
"We're very glad to notice
That you're going down our way."

Along they sauntered gaily,
Till on a wayside stone
They saw young Benny Beetle Bug
A-sitting there alone.
"Good-morning, Sir," they caroled.
"Good-morning all, to you,"
Said Benny, "are you traveling?
I'd like to travel, too."
They beckoned him politely;
He followed with a will.
And if they haven't stopped for tea
I think they're strolling still.

BARBARA YOUNG

THERE ONCE WAS A PUFFIN

Oh, there once was a Puffin
Just the shape of a muffin,
And he lived on an island
  In the
    bright
      blue
        sea!

He ate little fishes,
That were most delicious,
And he had them for supper
  And he
    had them
      for tea.

But this poor little Puffin,
He couldn't play nothin',
For he hadn't anybody
  To
    play
      with
        at all.

So he sat on his island,
And he cried for awhile, and
He felt very lonely,
  And he
    felt
      very
        small.

Then along came the fishes,
And they said, "If you wishes,
You can have us for playmates
  Instead
    of
      for
        tea!"

So they now play together,
In all sorts of weather,
And the Puffin eats pancakes,
  Like you
    and
      like
        me.

FLORENCE PAGE JAQUES

THE DUEL

The gingham dog and the calico cat
Side by side on the table sat;
'Twas half-past twelve, and (what do you think!)
Nor one nor t'other had slept a wink!
The old Dutch clock and the Chinese plate
Appeared to know as sure as fate
There was going to be a terrible spat.
*(I wasn't there; I simply state
What was told to me by the Chinese plate!)*

The gingham dog went, "Bow-wow-wow!"
And the calico cat replied, "Mee-ow!"
The air was littered, an hour or so,
With bits of gingham and calico,
While the old Dutch clock in the chimney place
Up with its hands before its face,
For it always dreaded a family row!
*(Now mind: I'm only telling you
What the old Dutch clock declares is true!)*

The Chinese plate looked very blue,
And wailed, "Oh, dear! what shall we do!"
But the gingham dog and the calico cat
Wallowed this way and tumbled that,
Employing every tooth and claw
In the awfullest way you ever saw—
And, oh! how the gingham and calico flew!
*(Don't fancy I exaggerate—
I got my news from the Chinese plate!)*

Next morning, where the two had sat,
They found no trace of dog or cat;
And some folks think unto this day
That burglars stole that pair away!
But the truth about the cat and pup
Is this: they ate each other up!
Now what do you really think of that!
*(The old Dutch clock it told me so,
And that is how I came to know.)*

EUGENE FIELD

I SAW A SHIP A-SAILING

I saw a ship a-sailing,
A-sailing on the sea;
And, oh! it was all laden
With pretty things for thee!

There were comfits in the cabin,
And apples in the hold.
The sails were all of silk,
And the masts were made of gold.

The four-and-twenty sailors
That stood between the decks,
Were four-and-twenty white mice,
With chains about their necks.

The captain was a duck,
With a packet on his back;
And when the ship began to move,
The captain said, "Quack! Quack!"

OLD RHYME

HE THOUGHT HE SAW

He thought he saw a Buffalo
Upon the chimney piece:
He looked again, and found it was
His Sister's Husband's Niece.
"Unless you leave this house!" he said,
"I'll send for the Police!"

He thought he saw a Rattlesnake
That questioned him in Greek:
He looked again, and found it was
The Middle of Next Week.
"The one thing I regret," he said,
"Is that it cannot speak!"

He thought he saw a Banker's Clerk
Descending from the bus:
He looked again, and found it was
A Hippopotamus:
"If this should stay to dine," he said,
"There won't be much for us!"

He thought he saw a Kangaroo
That worked a coffee mill:
He looked again, and found it was
A Vegetable-Pill.
"Were I to swallow this," he said,
"I should be very ill!"

He thought he saw a Coach-and-Four
That stood beside his bed:
He looked again, and found it was
A Bear without a Head.
"Poor thing," he said, "poor silly thing!
"It's waiting to be fed!"

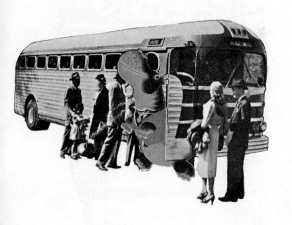

He thought he saw an Albatross
That fluttered round the lamp:
He looked again, and found it was
A Penny-Postage-Stamp.
"You'd best be getting home," he said:
"The nights are very damp!"

LEWIS CARROLL

MR. NOBODY

I know a funny little man,
　　As quiet as a mouse,
Who does the mischief that is done
　　In everybody's house!
There's no one ever sees his face,
　　And yet we all agree
That every plate we break was cracked
　　By Mr. Nobody.

'Tis he who always tears our books,
　　Who leaves the door ajar,
He pulls the buttons from our shirts,
　　And scatters pins afar;
That squeaking door will always squeak,
　　For, prithee, don't you see,
We leave the oiling to be done
　　By Mr. Nobody.

He puts damp wood upon the fire,
　　That kettles cannot boil;
His are the feet that bring in mud,
　　And all the carpets soil.
The papers always are mislaid,
　　Who had them last but he?
There's no one tosses them about
　　But Mr. Nobody.

The finger marks upon the door
　　By none of us are made;
We never leave the blinds unclosed,
　　To let the curtains fade.
The ink we never spill; the boots
　　That lying round you see
Are not our boots—they all belong
　　To Mr. Nobody.

AUTHOR UNKNOWN

MRS. SNIPKIN AND MRS. WOBBLECHIN

Skinny Mrs. Snipkin,
 With her little pipkin,
Sat by the fireside a-warming of her toes.
 Fat Mrs. Wobblechin,
 With her little doublechin,
Sat by the window a-cooling of her nose.

Says this one to that one,
 "Oh! you silly fat one,
Will you shut the window down?
You're freezing me to death!"
Says that one to t'other one,
 "Good gracious,
 how you bother one!
There isn't air enough for me
to draw my precious breath!"

Skinny Mrs. Snipkin,
Took her little pipkin,
Threw it straight across the room
 as hard as she could throw;
Hit Mrs. Wobblechin
On her little doublechin
 And out of the window
 a-tumble she did go.

LAURA E. RICHARDS

244

JONATHAN BING

Poor old Jonathan Bing
Went out in his carriage to visit the King,
But everyone pointed and said, "Look at that!
Jonathan Bing has forgotten his hat!"
        (He'd forgotten his hat!)

Poor old Jonathan Bing
Went home and put on a new hat for the King,
But by the palace a soldier said, "Hi!
You can't see the King; you've forgotten your tie!"
        (He'd forgotten his tie!)

Poor old Jonathan Bing,
He put on a beautiful tie for the King,
But when he arrived, an Archbishop said, "Ho!
You can't come to court in pajamas, you know!"

Poor old Jonathan Bing
Went home and addressed a short note to the King:
"If you please will excuse me, I won't come to tea;
For home's the best place for all people like me!"

BEATRICE CURTIS BROWN

THE RAGGEDY MAN

O the Raggedy Man! He works fer Pa;
An' he's the goodest man ever you saw!
He comes to our house every day,
An' waters the horses, an' feeds 'em hay;
An' he opens the shed—an' we all ist laugh
When he drives out our little old wobble-ly calf;
An' nen—ef our hired girl says he can—
He milks the cow fer 'Lizabuth Ann—
Ain't he a' awful good Raggedy Man?
    Raggedy! Raggedy! Raggedy Man!

Why, the Raggedy Man—he's ist so good
He splits the kindlin' an' chops the wood;
An' nen he spades in our garden, too,
An' does most things 'at *boys* can't do!—
He clumbed clean up in our big tree
An' shooked a' apple down fer me—
An' nother'n', too, fer 'Lizabuth Ann—
An' nother'n', too, fer the Raggedy Man—
Ain't he a' awful kind Raggedy Man?
    Raggedy! Raggedy! Raggedy Man!

An' the Raggedy Man, he knows most rhymes
An' tells 'em, ef I be good, sometimes;
Knows 'bout Giunts, an' Griffuns, an' Elves,
An' the Squidgicum-Squees 'at swallers therselves!
An' wite by the pump in our pasture-lot,
He showed me the hole 'at the Wunks is got,
'At lives 'way deep in the ground, an' can
Turn into me, er 'Lizabuth Ann!
Er Ma, er Pa, er the Raggedy Man!
Ain't he a funny old Raggedy Man?
    Raggedy! Raggedy! Raggedy Man!

The Raggedy Man—one time when he
Was makin' a little bow-'n'-arry fer me,
Says, "When *you're* big like your Pa is,
Air you go' to keep a fine store like his—
An' be a rich merchunt—an' wear fine clothes?—
Er what *air* you go' to be, goodness knows!"
An' nen he laughed at 'Lizabuth Ann,
An' I says, "'M go' to be a Raggedy Man!—
I'm ist go' to be a nice Raggedy Man!"
    Raggedy! Raggedy! Raggedy Man!

JAMES WHITCOMB RILEY

Pirate
Don Durk
of Dowdee

Ho, for the Pirate Don Durk of Dowdee!
He was as wicked as wicked could be,
But, oh, he was perfectly gorgeous to see!
    The Pirate Don Durk of Dowdee.

His conscience, of course, was as black as a bat,
But he had a floppety plume on his hat
And when he went walking it jiggled—like that!
    The plume of the Pirate Dowdee.

His coat it was handsome and cut with a slash,
And often as ever he twirled his mustache
Deep down in the ocean the mermaids went splash,
    Because of Don Durk of Dowdee.

Moreover, Dowdee had a purple tattoo,
And stuck in his belt where he buckled it through
Were a dagger, a dirk, and a squizzamaroo,
    For fierce was the Pirate Dowdee.

So fearful he was he would shoot at a puff,
And always at sea when the weather grew rough
He drank from a bottle and wrote on his cuff,
    Did Pirate Don Durk of Dowdee.

Oh, he had a cutlass that swung at his thigh
And he had a parrot called Pepperkin Pye,
And a zigzaggy scar at the end of his eye
    Had Pirate Don Durk of Dowdee.

He kept in a cavern, this buccaneer bold,
A curious chest that was covered with mould,
And all of his pockets were jingly with gold!
    Oh, jing! went the gold of Dowdee.

His conscience, of course, it was crook'd like a squash,
But both of his boots made a slickery slosh,
And he went through the world with a wonderful swash,
    Did Pirate Don Durk of Dowdee.

It's true he was wicked as wicked could be,
His sins they outnumbered a hundred and three,
But, oh, he was perfectly gorgeous to see,
    The Pirate Don Durk of Dowdee.

MILDRED PLEW MEIGS

LITTLE JOE TUNNEY

There was a little boy
And his name was Joe Tunney.
He had but one failing:
He tried to be funny.

He made himself noticed
In all public places
By making loud noises
And terrible faces.

One day at the circus
He wouldn't sit down.
He stood up and tried
To perform like a clown.

The clown said, "All right,
If you must jump and sing,
Come out with the show
And perform in the ring."

So out ran young Joe,
Acting foolish and wild,
And everyone watched him
But nobody smiled.

The actors all watched him,
The band loudly blared.
In dignified silence
The animals stared.

Thought poor little Joe,
Standing lonely and small,
"Oh, what shall I do?
I'm not funny at all!"

Then the elephant spoke
In the elephant tongue,
"I'll help that boy out—
After all, he's so young."

And he lifted Joe up
With his trunk in the air
And with one mighty sweep
Put him back in his chair.

The people all clapped
And the clowns cheered for Joe,
And he kept very still
For the rest of the show.

REBECCA MCCANN

THE CAVE BOY

I dreamed I was a cave boy
  And lived in a cave,
A mammoth for my saddle horse,
  A monkey for my slave.
And through the tree-fern forests
  A-riding I would go,
When I was once a cave boy,
  A million years ago.

I dreamed I was a cave boy;
  I hunted with a spear
The saber-toothèd tiger,
  The prehistoric deer.
A wolfskin for my dress suit,
  I thought me quite a beau,
When I was once a cave boy,
  A million years ago.

I dreamed I was a cave boy;
    My dinner was a bone,
And how I had to fight for it,
    To get it for my own!
We banged each other o'er the head,
    And oft our blood did flow,
When I was once a cave boy,
    A million years ago.

I dreamed I was a cave boy.
    The torches' smoky light
Shone on the dinner table,
    A pile of bones so white.
I lapped some water from the spring,
    The easiest way, you know,
When I was once a cave boy,
    A million years ago.

I dreamed—but now I am awake;
    A voice is in my ear.
"Come out and have a game of ball!
    The sun is shining clear.
We'll have some doughnuts afterwards,
    And then a-swimming go!"
I'm glad I'm *not* a cave boy,
    A million years ago!

LAURA E. RICHARDS

253

THE SUGAR-PLUM TREE

Have you ever heard of the Sugar-Plum Tree?
    'Tis a marvel of great renown!
It blooms on the shore of the Lollipop Sea
    In the garden of Shut-Eye Town;
The fruit that it bears is so wondrously sweet
    (As those who have tasted it say)
That good little children have only to eat
    Of that fruit to be happy next day.

When you've got to the tree, you would have a hard time
    To capture the fruit which I sing;
The tree is so tall that no person could climb
    To the boughs where the sugar-plums swing!
But up in that tree sits a chocolate cat,
    And a gingerbread dog prowls below—
And this is the way you contrive to get at
    Those sugar-plums tempting you so:

You say but the word to that gingerbread dog
    And he barks with such terrible zest
That the chocolate cat is at once all agog,
    As her swelling proportions attest.
And the chocolate cat goes cavorting around
    From this leafy limb unto that,
And the sugar-plums tumble, of course, to the ground—
    Hurrah for that chocolate cat!

There are marshmallows, gumdrops, and peppermint canes,
    With stripings of scarlet and gold,
And you carry away of the treasure that rains
    As much as your apron can hold!
So come, little child, cuddle closer to me
    In your dainty white nightcap and gown,
And I'll rock you away to that Sugar-Plum Tree
    In the garden of Shut-Eye Town.

EUGENE FIELD

WYNKEN, BLYNKEN, AND NOD

Wynken, Blynken, and Nod one night
Sailed off in a wooden shoe—
Sailed on a river of crystal light
    Into a sea of dew.
"Where are you going, and what do you wish?"
The old moon asked the three.
"We have come to fish for the herring fish
    That live in this beautiful sea;
    Nets of silver and gold have we!"
      Said Wynken,
      Blynken,
      And Nod.

The old moon laughed and sang a song,
As they rocked in the wooden shoe,
And the wind that sped them all night long
    Ruffled the waves of dew.
The little stars were the herring fish
That lived in that beautiful sea—
"Now cast your nets wherever you wish—
    Never afeard are we!"
So cried the stars to the fishermen three:
      Wynken,
      Blynken,
      And Nod.

All night long their nets they threw
To the stars in the twinkling foam—
Then down from the skies came the wooden shoe,
        Bringing the fishermen home;
'Twas all so pretty a sail it seemed
As if it could not be,
And some folks thought 'twas a dream they'd dreamed
        Of sailing that beautiful sea—
        But I shall name you the fishermen three:
            Wynken,
            Blynken,
            And Nod.

Wynken and Blynken are two little eyes,
And Nod is a little head,
And the wooden shoe that sailed the skies
        Is a wee one's trundle-bed.
So shut your eyes while mother sings
Of wonderful sights that be,
And you shall see the beautiful things
        As you rock in the misty sea
Where the old shoe rocked the fishermen three:
            Wynken,
            Blynken,
            And Nod.

EUGENE FIELD

THE LITTLE HOUSE

In a great big wood in a great big tree
There's the nicest little house that could possibly be.

There's a tiny little knocker on the tiny little door,
And a tiny little carpet on the tiny little floor;

There's a tiny little table, and a tiny little bed,
And a tiny little pillow for a tiny *weeny* head;

A tiny little blanket, and a tiny little sheet,
And a tiny water bottle (hot) for tiny little feet.

A tiny little eiderdown; a tiny little chair;
And a tiny little kettle for the owner
(when he's there).

In a tiny little larder there's a tiny thermos bottle
For a tiny little greedy man who knows the
Woods of Pottle.

There's a tiny little peg for a tiny little hat,
And a tiny little dog and a tiny *tiny* cat.

If you've got a little house
And you keep it spick and span,
Perhaps there'll come to live in it
A tiny little man.
You may not ever see him
(He is extremely shy):
But if you find a crumpled sheet,
Or pins upon the window seat,
Or see the marks of tiny feet
You'll know the reason why.

ELIZABETH GODLEY

25

SOMETIMES

Some days are fairy days.
  The minute that you wake
You have a magic feeling
  that you never could mistake;
You may not see the fairies,
  but you know that they're about,
And any single minute they
  might all come popping out;
You want to laugh, you want to sing,
  you want to dance and run,
Everything is different,
  everything is fun;
The sky is full of fairy clouds,
  the streets are fairy ways—
Anything might happen
  on truly fairy days.

Some nights are fairy nights.
  Before you go to bed
You hear their darling music
  go chiming in your head;
You look into the garden,
  and through the misty grey
You see the trees all waiting
  in a breathless kind of way.
All the stars are smiling;
  they know that very soon
The fairies will come singing
  from the land behind the moon.
If only you could keep awake
  when Nurse puts out the light . . .
Anything might happen
  on a truly fairy night.

ROSE FYLEMAN

THE FAIRIES

Up the airy mountain,
  Down the rushy glen,
We daren't go a-hunting,
  For fear of little men;
Wee folk, good folk,
  Trooping all together;
Green jacket, red cap,
  And white owl's feather!

Down along the rocky shore
  Some make their home,
They live on crispy pancakes
  Of yellow tide-foam;
Some in the reeds
  Of the black mountain lake,
With frogs for their watchdogs,
  All night awake.

WILLIAM ALLINGHAM

THE GOBLIN

A goblin lives in *our* house, in *our* house, in *our* house,
A goblin lives in *our* house all the year round.
      He bumps
      And he jumps
      And he thumps
      And he stumps.
      He knocks
      And he rocks
And he rattles at the locks.
A goblin lives in *our* house, in *our* house, in *our* house,
A goblin lives in *our* house all the year round.

ROSE FYLEMAN

Oh, who is so merry, so merry, heigh ho!
As the light-hearted fairy? heigh ho,
 Heigh ho!
  He dances and sings
  To the sound of his wings,
With a hey and a heigh and a ho!

Oh, who is so merry, so airy, heigh ho!
As the light-hearted fairy? heigh ho,
 Heigh ho!
  His nectar he sips
  From the primroses' lips,
With a hey and a heigh and a ho!

Oh, who is so merry, so merry, heigh ho!
As the light-hearted fairy? heigh ho!
 Heigh ho!
  The night is his noon
  And his sun is the moon,
With a hey and a heigh and a ho!

AUTHOR UNKNOWN

THE LIGHT-HEARTED FAIRY

THE BEST GAME THE FAIRIES PLAY

The best game the fairies play,
 The best game of all,
Is sliding down steeples—
 (You know they're very tall).
You fly to the weathercock,
 And when you hear it crow
You fold your wings and clutch your things
 And then let go!

They have a million other games—
 Cloud-catching's one,
And mud-mixing after rain
 Is heaps and heaps of fun;
But when you go and stay with them
 Never mind the rest,
Take my advice—they're very nice,
 But steeple-sliding's best!

ROSE FYLEMAN

A FAIRY WENT A-MARKETING

A fairy went a-marketing—
  She bought a little fish;
She put it in a crystal bowl
  Upon a golden dish.
An hour she sat in wonderment
  And watched its silver gleam,
And then she gently took it up
  And slipped it in a stream.

A fairy went a-marketing—
  She bought a colored bird;
It sang the sweetest, shrillest song
  That ever she had heard.
She sat beside the painted cage
  And listened half the day,
And then she opened wide the door
  And let it fly away.

A fairy went a-marketing—
  She bought a winter gown
All stitched about with gossamer
  And lined with thistledown.
She wore it all afternoon
  With prancing and delight,
Then gave it to a little frog
  To keep him warm at night.

A fairy went a-marketing—
  She bought a gentle mouse
To take her tiny messages,
  To keep her tiny house.
All day she kept its busy feet
  Pit-patting to and fro,
And then she kissed its silken ears,
  Thanked it, and let it go.

ROSE FYLEMAN

overheard on a saltmarsh

Nymph, nymph, what are your beads?
Green glass, goblin. Why do you stare at them?
Give them me.

      No.

Give them me. Give them me.

      No.

Then I will howl all night in the reeds,
Lie in the mud and howl for them.

Goblin, why do you love them so?

They are better than stars or water,
Better than voices of winds that sing,
Better than any man's fair daughter,
Your green glass beads on a silver ring.

Hush, I stole them out of the moon.

Give me your beads, I desire them.

      No.

I will howl in a deep lagoon
For your green glass beads, I love them so.
Give them me. Give them.

      No.

HAROLD MONRO

I met a little Elf man, once,
Down where the lilies blow.
I asked him why he was so small,
And why he didn't grow.

He slightly frowned, and with his eye
He looked me through and through.
"I'm quite as big for me," said he,
"As you are big for you!"

JOHN KENDRICK BANGS

the little elf

the elf and the dormouse

Under a toadstool crept a wee Elf
Out of the rain to shelter himself.

Under the toadstool, sound asleep,
Sat a big Dormouse all in a heap.

Trembled the wee Elf, frightened, and yet
Fearing to fly away lest he get wet.

To the next shelter—maybe a mile!
Sudden the wee Elf smiled a wee smile.

Tugged till the toadstool toppled in two.
Holding it over him, gaily he flew.

Soon he was safe home, dry as could be.
Soon woke the Dormouse—"Good gracious me!

"Where is my toadstool?" loud he lamented
—And that's how umbrellas first were invented.

OLIVER HERFORD

SOME ONE

Some one came knocking
At my wee, small door;
Some one came knocking,
I'm sure—sure—sure;
I listened, I opened,
I looked to left and right,
But nought there was a-stirring
In the still dark night;
Only the busy beetle
Tap-tapping in the wall,
Only from the forest
The screech-owl's call,
Only the cricket whistling
While the dewdrops fall,
So I know not who came knocking,
At all, at all, at all.

WALTER DE LA MARE

Prayers

Psalm 100

Make a joyful noise unto the Lord, all ye lands.
Serve the Lord with gladness:
Come before His presence with singing.

Know ye that the Lord He is God:
It is He that hath made us, and not we ourselves;
We are His people, and the sheep of His pasture.

Enter into His gates with thanksgiving,
And into His courts with praise:
Be thankful unto Him, and bless His name.

For the Lord is good;
His mercy is everlasting;
And His truth endureth to all generations.

THE BIBLE

Old Gaelic Lullaby

Hush! the waves are rolling in,
White with foam, white with foam.
Father toils amid the din,
But baby sleeps at home.

Hush! the winds roar hoarse and deep!
On they come, on they come!
Brother seeks the wandering sheep,
But baby sleeps at home.

Hush! the rain sweeps o'er the knowes
Where they roam, where they roam
Sister goes to seek the cows,
But baby sleeps at home

FATHER OF ALL

Father of all, in Heaven above,
We thank Thee for Thy love;
Our food, our home, and all we wear
Tell of Thy loving care.

THANK YOU

Thank You for the world so sweet,
Thank You for the food we eat,
Thank You for the birds that sing,
Thank You, God, for everything.

MRS. E. RUTTER LEATHAN

272

FATHER, WE THANK THEE

For flowers that bloom about our feet,
Father, we thank Thee,
For tender grass so fresh and sweet,
Father, we thank Thee,
For song of bird and hum of bee,
For all things fair we hear or see,
Father in heaven, we thank Thee.

For blue of stream and blue of sky,
Father, we thank Thee,
For pleasant shade of branches high,
Father, we thank Thee,
For fragrant air and cooling breeze,
For beauty of the blooming trees,
Father in heaven, we thank Thee.

AUTHOR UNKNOWN

FOR THIS NEW MORNING

For this new morning and its light,
For rest and shelter of the night,
For health and food, for love and friends,
For every gift His goodness sends
We thank Thee, gracious Lord. Amen.

FOR THE NIGHT

Father, we thank Thee for the night,
And for the pleasant morning light;
For rest and food and loving care,
And all that makes the day so fair.
Help us to do the things we should,
To be to others kind and good;
In all we do, all we say,
To grow more loving every day.

DEAR LORD, FOR THESE THREE THINGS I PRAY

Dear Lord, for these three things I pray:
To know Thee more clearly,
To love Thee more dearly,
To follow Thee more nearly,
Every day.

VESPERS

Little Boy kneels at the foot of the bed,
Droops on the little hands little gold head.
Hush! Hush! Whisper who dares!
Christopher Robin is saying his prayers.

God bless Mummy. I know that's right.
Wasn't it fun in the bath tonight?
The cold's so cold, and the hot's so hot.
Oh! *God bless Daddy*—I quite forgot.

If I open my fingers a little bit more,
I can see Nanny's dressing gown on the door.
It's a beautiful blue, but it hasn't a hood.
Oh! *God bless Nanny and make her good.*

Mine has a hood, and I lie in bed,
And pull the hood right over my head,
And I shut my eyes, and I curl up small,
And nobody knows that I'm there at all.

Oh! *Thank you, God, for a lovely day.*
And what was the other I had to say?
I said, "Bless Daddy," so what can it be?
Oh! Now I remember it. *God bless Me.*

Little Boy kneels at the foot of the bed,
Droops on the little hands little gold head.
Hush! Hush! Whisper who dares!
Christopher Robin is saying his prayers.

A. A. MILNE

Illustration Acknowledgments

The publishers of CHILDCRAFT gratefully acknowledge the courtesy of the following artists, photographers, publishers, agencies, and corporations for illustrations in this volume. Page numbers refer to two-page spreads. The words "(*left*)," "(*center*)," "(*top*)," "(*bottom*)," and "(*right*)," indicate position on the spread. Names marked with an asterisk (°) indicate that illustration is the exclusive property of the publishers of CHILDCRAFT.

MOTHER GOOSE AND NURSERY RHYMES:

8–9: Sylvia Sullivan (°)
10–11: art by Eloise Wilkin (°); photo, courtesy Tell City Chair Company
12–13: art by Eloise Wilkin (°); photo by Ormond Gigli, courtesy Metropolitan Life Insurance Company
14–15: (*left*) B. Pinsley, Alpha Photo Associates, Inc.; (*right*) Michael Peirce
16–17: Susan Perl (°)
18–19: Josef A. Schneider
20–21: art by Vernon McKissack (°); photo, courtesy Arkansas Industrial Development Commission
22–23: courtesy Gerber Products Company
24–25: (*top*) Fred Meyer (°); (*bottom*) Suzi Hawes (°)
26–27: art by Gordon Kwiatkowski (°); photo, Authenticated News
28–29: Fred Meyer (°)
30–31: photo by Walter Chandoha; art by Elizabeth Schon (°)
32–33: Vernon McKissack (°)
34–35: Garth Williams (°)
36–37: (*left*) Russell Jackson (°); (*right*) Russell Jackson, courtesy Dept. of Conservation, State of Indiana
38–39: Susan Perl (°)
40–41: (*left*) Henry C. Pitz (°); (*right*) Leonard Weisgard (°)
42–43: art by Robert Kresin (°); photography by Mel Kaspar (°)
44–45: Vernon McKissack (°)
46–47: Gyo Fujikawa (°)
48–49: Leonard Weisgard (°)
50–51: art by Eloise Wilkin (°); photo by Erika Schmachtenberger, Bildberichterstattung, courtesy of *Deutschland Revue*
52: Tana Hoban, courtesy Carrier Corporation

POEMS FOR OUTDOORS:

53: Russell Jackson (°)
54–55: Mary Horton (°)
56–57: Charles Reiche, Scope Associates
58–59: Mary Horton (°)
60–61: art by Mary Horton (°); photo by Douglas Kirkland
62–63: art by Mary Horton (°); photo by Frank Fenner (°)
64–65: Mary Horton (°)
66–67: Mary Horton (°)
68–69: photo from F.P.G.
70–71: art by Gordon Kwiatkowski (°); photo by Dorothy McLaughlin, Arizona Photographic Associates
72–73: Mary Horton (°)
74–75: (*left*) Susan Perl (°); (*right*) art by Elizabeth Orton Jones (°); photo, Herman Eisenbeiss, Photo Researchers
76–77: photo from Yerkes Observatory; art by Mary Horton (°)
78–79: (*left*) H. Armstrong Roberts; (*right*) Luoma Photos
80–81: Mary Horton (°)
82–83: (*left, top and bottom right*) photographs from *The Shadow Book* by Beatrice Schenk de Regniers, photographs © 1960 by Isabel Gordon, reproduced by permission of Harcourt, Brace & World, Inc.; (*center*) Alfred Eisenstaedt, courtesy *LIFE*, © 1959 Time Inc.
84–85: Art Kane
86–87: photo by John H. Atkinson, Jr., Alpha Photo Associates, Inc.; art by Elizabeth Schon (°)
88–89: painting by Esther Seymour Stevenson (a detail)
90–91: photo by Carroll Seghers II, © The Cream of Wheat Corp.; art by Eloise Wilkin (°)
92–93: John Henry—Stephens Biondi De Cicco Inc. (°)
94–95: art by Paul McNear (°); photo, courtesy © Florida Citrus Commission
96–97: Mary Miller Salem (°)
98–99: photo by Cole, Monkmeyer; art by Susan Perl (°)
100: Dick Smith

POEMS ABOUT PLANTS AND ANIMALS:

101: Russell Jackson (°)
102–103: (*left*) Walt Langenberg, from *U.S. Camera*; (*right*) Walter Chandoha
104–105: art by Gordon Laite (°); photo by Gene Daniels, Black Star Publishing Co., Inc.
106–107: Fred Womack (°)
108–109: (*left*) Mary Hauge (°); (*right*) Garth Williams (°)
110–111: (*top*) Garth Williams (°); (*bottom*) Vernon McKissack (°)
112–113: photo by Grant Heilman; art by Neal Cochran (°)
114–115: art by Clark Bruorton (°); photography by Frank Cassidy (°)
116–117: Gordon Laite (°)
118–119: Garth Williams (°)
120–121: art by Vernon McKissack (°)
122–123: Gyo Fujikawa (°)
124–125: (*left*) Eraldo Carugati and (*right*) Andy Aldrige —Stephens Biondi De Cicco Inc. (°)
126: Dorothy McLaughlin, Arizona Photographic Associates

RHYMES OF LIFE AT HOME:

127: Russell Jackson (°)
128–129: Lee Rossow—Stephens Biondi De Cicco Inc. (°)
130–131: Susan Perl (°)
132–133: Meg Wohlberg (°)
134–135: photo, courtesy American Viscose Corporation; art by Clark Bruorton (°)
136–137: photography by Mel Kaspar (°); art by Clark Bruorton (°)
138–139: (*left*) courtesy Metropolitan Life Insurance Co.; (*right*) art by Vanides Design (°), photo by Torkel Korling
140–141: (*left*) Mary Horton (°); (*right*) Alaine Johnson
142–143: Mary Horton (°)
144–145: (*left*) painting "La Toilette" by Mary Cassatt, courtesy The Art Institute of Chicago; (*right*) Clark Bruorton (°)
146–147: Mary Horton (°)
148: Harold Halma, courtesy of Gerber Products Co.

POEMS OF PLAY AND MAKE-BELIEVE:

149: Russell Jackson (°)
150–151: (*left*) Zehrt, F.P.G.; (*right*) Dorothy McLaughlin, Arizona Photographic Associates
152–153: (*left*) Dorothy McLaughlin, Arizona Photographic Associates; (*right*) painting by Mia Carpenter, courtesy of Joseph Love INC.
154–155: Meg Wohlberg (°)
156–157: Dorothy McLaughlin, Arizona Photographic Associates
158–159: photo, courtesy of the First 3 Markets Group— the Sunday Magazine Section of *The New York News, Chicago Tribune*, and *Philadelphia Inquirer*; art by Susan Perl (°)
160–161: William Pène du Bois (°)
162–163: (*left*) Dorothy McLaughlin, Arizona Photographic Associates; (*right*) courtesy *GMAC TIME PAYMENT PLAN*
164–165: art by Mary Miller Salem (°); photo by J. Schneider, F.P.G.
166–167: art by Susan Perl (°); photo by Don Boose, Alpha Photo Associates, Inc.

Author Index

Use this index if you know only the author of the poem. The Title Index will be found on page 282 and the First Line Index on page 286.

Title Index

Use this index if you know only the title of the poem. The Author Index will be found on page 279 and the First Line Index on page 286.

285

Index of First Lines

Use this index if you know only the first line of the poem. The Author Index will be found on page 279 and the Title Index on page 282.

288